MW01118026

A PIGEON
AMONG
THE CATS

A PIGEON
AMONG
THE CATS

JOSEPHINE BELL

STEIN AND DAY/*Publishers*/New York

First published in the United States of America, 1977
Copyright © 1974 by D.B. Ball
All rights reserved
Printed in the United States of America
Stein and Day/*Publishers*/Scarborough House,
Briarcliff Manor, N.Y. 10510
ISBN 0-8128-2411-3

Chapter I

MRS. LAWLER STEPPED out of the plane at Genoa Airport to breathe deeply the bright warm air of Italy. This was what she had come for; to lose the cold grey blanket settled so firmly over her for more than a month. She had thought she would never get rid of it or be able to wear the summer clothes that had been scarcely touched for the whole of that so-called summer in England. Friends had warned her it would be far too hot in Italy in August: not a bit of it, she told herself half an hour later as she left the airport buildings again, directed by a pleasant fresh-faced young woman, who ticked her name off on a card she held while she explained that the coach was waiting to take them on the first stage of their tour.

Mrs. Lawler moved out into the sunshine again and looked about her. Half a dozen coaches were waiting: the tourist trade at full stretch evidently. Carefully remembering what she had been told, she moved towards one of the monsters of the correct colour and name. 'Roseanna' was scrawled sideways across the wide stern. The name of her tour company was written below and to the side. 'Roseanna' was a name Mrs. Lawler was always to remember.

As she moved unhurriedly towards the coach, for she had little hand luggage and knew just enough Italian to help her past the initial difficulties, she found someone at her elbow, panting a little, asking in a very hesitant voice, "Are you for the Queensway tour by any chance?"

"I believe there are two or even three," Mrs. Lawler said, looking round. "I was told mine is called 'Roseanna', but there is one for Naples after Rome. The brochure gave one for the Lakes as well."

As the young woman beside her swung away again, as if to find a less complicated answer, Mrs. Lawler went on, "I am going to Rome and then Florence and Venice. That is by this coach here, 'Roseanna'."

But the impatient young woman had gone, so Mrs. Lawler presented her ticket to the coach driver who did not want to see it, but flashed a fine row of teeth at her and waved his hand over the interior of the coach, inviting her to choose a seat.

This she did, directly behind him, which gave her an excellent view through the windscreen as well as out of the side window. How pleasant, she thought, to have all the luggage problems settled for you. As long as it works, she reminded herself. But as the driver jumped down at that moment to receive a load of suitcases for the party among which she saw her own, she abandoned the last shred of responsibility for the time being.

The rest of her fellow travellers arrived in a solid mass directly afterwards. Why so much later than herself, Mrs. Lawler wondered? The loo, too scared to manage on the plane? Not all of them, surely? There had been a queue, which she had herself joined. No, but several with various Italian foods, already nibbling. No children, thank God, in our lot. There had been one or two shouters and whiners during the flight.

"May I sit beside you?"

Mrs. Lawler found it was the scatty young woman again, looking at her from the central aisle with a pleading expression.

"Of course. Would you like to be by the window?"

The young woman looked startled.

6

"No, no, of course not. Don't move. I'll put my coat on the rack. I suppose our luggage has come over?"

"I saw it arrive. I wondered too. I'm not used to having everything done for me. Quite the reverse."

"Really?"

Mrs. Lawler did not explain further. She foresaw many speeding miles during which life stories would be exchanged. Worse than on board a ship, she thought. There you could at least get up after a short interval and walk about. Here you were committed for several hours at a time.

Before the end of that day Mrs. Lawler found that the seats her partners in travel had chosen that morning were by common, unspoken agreement considered fixed. She was landed with this young woman and would have to make the best of it. While moving, at any rate.

Not that much conversation was needed to begin with, for the road out of Genoa was exciting, spectacular, winding its ingenious, level, breathtaking way through tunnels, across bridges, round corners where the sea flashed blue for a few seconds or the next door dual-carriageway poured out its own quota of cars just before theirs was swallowed up by the same tunnel's mouth.

Mrs. Lawler glanced at the figure beside her. The girl, she had appeared no more at the airport, looked rather older now, but perhaps no more than thirty, was staring straight in front of her, both hands clutching the little rail the driver had put up between his sprung seat and the passengers. She seemed to notice Mrs. Lawler's eye upon her, for she turned slowly and gave her a shy smile.

"Isn't it a wonderful road?" she said.

"The Italians have always been good engineers," Mrs. Lawler answered. It was insufferably smug and condescending to say such a thing, she knew. Also far less than she felt. The girl turned her face back to the road. She did not speak again.

At Pisa the coach put them off to see the sights: three

white masses glittering in the sunshine, milled about by tourists in bright clothes and faced by a long row of incredibly vulgar stalls, displaying towers that leaned on every possible material, from heavy dishes to wooden soup bowls, to artificial silk scarves to toy animals, to flags, to combs, to pipes, to guitars, to hats, to shirts, to leather purses.

Walking off rapidly by herself, with her camera dangling, but without much intention of using it, Mrs. Lawler made for the private burial ground and its cloister, avoiding the church, the baptistry and the tower, that she had no wish to climb. In the "campo" she did find all and more than she expected and spent a happy half-hour browsing among the inscriptions ancient and modern upon the tombs she found there.

She was recalled to the coach by the courier who gave her name as Billie. They would stay in Pisa for the night and it was time to go to their hotel to sort themselves out, Billie said.

Mrs. Lawler made no objection to this. The day had meant a very early start in England and had been tiring, though she felt she had done nothing. Still, that had been the object of the exercise, her friends had told her.

At dinner that evening Mrs. Lawler sat at a table for four. The others were a father, mother and young daughter all called Banks. They came from the Midlands and had travelled to Gatwick the night before. They were properly whacked, Mrs. Banks said and she for one dreaded the early start they were to make the next day. Mr. Banks said that didn't apply to him, he was used to long hours travelling. Miss Banks did not say anything. She did not eat much, either. She pushed the food about her plate, swung her long straight hair out of her eyes, fiddled with the fringe on a leather shawl she wore half on and half off one shoulder, but apart from these movements seemed to have very little contact with the world about her. Certainly not with Mrs. Lawler, who ate heartily and found

8

herself abandoned while she was still occupied with a large bunch of succulent grapes.

On her way from the dining room she passed her coach companion carrying a cup of coffee from the bar where she had collected it towards a sofa chair in the lounge, where a youngish couple were beckoning to her.

"We shall be sorting ourselves out tomorrow," Mrs. Lawler told herself, hopefully.

But she was wrong. Though at breakfast she found herself beside a stout elderly woman and her niece, when she climbed into the coach she found the front seat again empty, passed by, avoided, until the thin girl slipped into it again just before Billie took her courier's place, greeted them all and began to explain the plan for the day.

"I hope you had time for breakfast," Mrs. Lawler said to her companion. "I didn't see you come down."

"I never have breakfast," the girl said. She wore her worried look again.

Mrs. Lawler was vaguely alarmed, but she told herself firmly it was none of her business and found nothing much better to say than, "I still don't know your name, I'm afraid. I am Rose Lawler, retired schoolmistress," she added, in a half joking voice to suggest she no longer wielded authority.

The girl turned to stare at her.

"But you're married," she protested.

"I was." Mrs. Lawler was used to this response, not always expressed so immediately nor so openly. "A long time ago," she explained with patient forbearance. "In the war — he was killed not long afterwards. I had taught before the war, so I taught again. I retired last year. And you?"

"Me?"

"You are married, I see."

"Oh! Oh, yes. Of course! Gwen, that's my name. Gwen Chilton."

To Mrs. Lawler's horror her companion fumbled for a

9

handkerchief and dabbed at tears. Or dust, perhaps. Mario, the driver, had wound down the window beside him to cool one large hand, which he hung out of it from time to time. Personally Mrs. Lawler enjoyed the warm draught, but perhaps...

"No, it's all right," Mrs. Chilton assured her. She put away the handkerchief, smiled once or twice and said, "You see it was hearing you were a widow and had — well — managed so well. You see —" she began to fumble again.

"You aren't going to tell me you've lost your husband, too?"

Mrs. Lawler was aghast. She could not stop what was coming. It was already dropping into Mrs. Chilton's lap, so to speak, but it was not, most surely not, what she had expected. Get over the boredom of idleness with a lot of silly people on their annual holiday. She had doubted the travel agent's word. She had been right. There was nothing she could say now that would not make matters worse. So she turned her head away from the weeping girl beside her and tried to enjoy the countryside that flowed past the coach and spread itself in front of them, while Mrs. Chilton jerked out her misery in small parcels of words.

"I haven't lost him... I mean he's alive all right... but we don't get on... he has other girls at the office and that. I stood it a long time... fool I was, I think. They don't alter if they're made that way, do they?... So I made up my mind to end it... There weren't any children... It was more than flesh and blood could stand."

In one of the longer pauses in this dreary recital Mrs. Lawler thought, with sickening disgust, it might be a radio play. She's got every last cliché and trite complaint, poor bitch! And then felt ashamed of herself, but still lacking in true feeling.

"So I've run out on him," Mrs. Chilton was saying. "I couldn't stand it. I took every penny I could find in

10

the house and my summer things and booked at the last minute."

"But didn't leave word where you had gone?"

"No. I didn't leave word of any kind."

"But someone knows where you are? I mean you have telephoned once or twice, haven't you?"

Mrs. Chilton did not seem to have heard this question but when Mrs. Lawler repeated it she said grudgingly, "Well yes, I did phone my best friend. But no one in my family — or his."

Confusion had improved Mrs. Chilton. When the coach stopped for morning coffee at a wayside cafeteria near a petrol station Mrs. Lawler saw to it that her companion had a large cappuccino and a packet of biscuits, which she ate steadily and completely.

Thereafter the conversation took a brighter turn. Mrs. Lawler explained why she was a retired school mistress. She had begun to teach just before the start of the Second World War, then had been called up and went into the W.A.A.F. She married into the Air Force, her husband was brought down over the Channel, badly wounded, he died later, she went back into teaching when she was demobilised.

"You never married again?" Mrs. Chilton asked in an astonished voice.

"No, I never married again."

"And no children, either?"

"One son, born after his father's death. He went to Canada six years ago."

Mrs. Chilton glanced sideways at her companion, but finding a closed expression there, did not ask any more questions.

The coach stopped for that day at an hotel in Siena. It was by then a little after four o'clock with the shops coming to life again after the universal siesta break. When the rooms at the hotel had been allocated and the luggage delivered to them most of the tourists hurried out to look

11

at the shops, buy postcards, cigarettes and stamps in the last available minutes of the commercial day. Or to see the sights.

Mrs. Lawler stood at the foot of the hotel steps, an open map in her hand, trying to orientate herself. Various other fellow travellers hovered near her, murmuring their ignorance and pleading indirectly for enlightenment.

"I'm trying to locate the duomo, the cathedral," said Mrs. Lawler firmly, aloud. "The Donatello statue of John the Baptist is there. And the big square, the Campo, at any rate."

A polite voice just behind her said, "I can help you if I may."

She looked over her shoulder. A man stood on the pavement. His face was on a level with hers, until she stepped down to the pavement when he proved to be a little taller. He was smiling, which made his crooked face look comic, rather than grotesque. He seemed to have been walking past the hotel and must have heard her complaint just as he reached her.

"Can you really?" Mrs. Lawler said, smiling back. "I'd be very grateful."

"Come on, then," the man said, still smiling. "I'm going in that direction, myself."

They moved away together. Before long Mrs. Lawler realised that she had Mrs. Chilton on her other side and behind them a young couple whose name she had gathered was Woodruff. But her guide was explaining some of the history of Siena and pointing out various buildings, so she bent her mind towards understanding him, deciding she had no obligation towards the others. It just crossed her mind that the kind man with his scarred face — was it old war-time burns — and his cultured English accent and his extensive local knowledge might presently demand a guide's fee, but she put the unworthy thought from her and continued to concentrate on her sightseeing.

12

No bill was presented, no fee was remotely suggested. With the cathedral in sight the man halted, took leave, accepted verbal gratitude and then turned to go back the way they had come.

"Oh dear," said Mrs. Lawler, "you have come right out of your way."

"Not really." The smile was in place, broader, more comical than ever. "I'm just wandering over well-remembered tracks."

They said goodbye; Mrs Lawler walked on into the church, where Mrs. Chilton drew level and the Woodruffs passed with a nod of recognition as if they had only just noticed who she was.

"That was a pretty cool customer, I must say," Mrs. Chilton remarked. "Or did you know him?"

"Never seen him from Adam," Mrs. Lawler answered. "He very kindly directed me here. He knows Siena and was just strolling round the place."

She was aware that her companion became rather more than rather less curious as a result of this speech and also that all her own vague misgivings had entered Mrs. Chilton's mind already. But she had no intention of sharing them with the girl. With her own friends at home she would have enjoyed inventing scurrilous tales to account for her brief acquaintance with a fellow countryman, but not with Gwen Chilton, whose mind ran on rather different lines, apparently.

However, they left the cathedral together and when they came to a broad flight of steps that led down into the wide square and Mrs. Lawler stopped to take a photograph of it, she heard a familiar voice say to Gwen, "A wonderful square, isn't it? They still have the old mediaeval horse race here every summer. We've missed it, I'm afraid. Last month."

Gwen answered, "Oh, really!" and Mrs. Lawler swung round, fastening up her camera in time to see the stranger's

13

back as he moved away again. Gwen said, sourly, "Worse than a guide book, isn't he?"

When Mrs. Lawler made no answer to this Gwen went on, "What's the matter with his face, anyhow?"

At this Mrs. Lawler could not help saying, "Burns, I think. He may have been in the Air Force in the war. I've seen a lot of that sort of thing."

Mrs. Chilton thought, Burns, my foot! Car crash, more likely. She's got the Air Force on the-brain, poor old cow. Pathetic. Teaching all her life except that one break!

Neither of them gave any more thought to the strange friendly man as they wandered down the steps to the square, sat in the shade at one side to eat a delicious ice-cream and wandered back to the hotel, where Mrs. Lawler unpacked a few things for the night, undressed, showered and dressed again in a thinner summer frock. She went down to the bar in good time to meet some more of her group before dinner. It was time to get to know a few more of them. A diet of Gwen Chilton, however sorry she felt for the girl, was not to be taken without relief.

She drank an apéritif with the Woodruffs. Conversation was simple; it consisted of a long account from Mr. Woodruff of his growing success in electronics. He spoke a type of Midlands cockney that mirrored this process exactly, so that when she asked Mrs. Woodruff where they lived in England the answer was Harrogate and she congratulated herself for a good guess.

At the meal she was joined by the woman and niece of breakfast that morning; the one too stout and the other too thin, as in a cartoon, but dressed alike, though not actually "twin" in flowered nylon, knee length, sleeveless. Mrs. Franks was a midwife, attached to a rare private maternity home in a London suburb. Miss Hurry was a state-registered nurse, taking a holiday abroad with her aunt before going to a new post in a provincial hospital. They had visited Spain twice, they explained, and wanted a change. Sunbathing was all very well in its way, but...

"I'm here to see Florence and Venice," Mrs. Lawler said gently.

"Not Rome?" Miss Hurry was surprised.

"I spent a week in Rome some years ago," Mrs. Lawler explained. "But Florence and Venice never yet. Time slips away so."

She sighed for all the plans made and never brought off, for one reason or another.

Gwen Chilton waylaid her on the way from the dining room.

"Going to have coffee?" she asked.

"Yes, that would be nice." Mrs. Lawler turned to invite her eating companions to join them but they had already disappeared.

"They make it at the bar," Gwen said, leading off in that direction.

But Mrs. Lawler had stopped at the middle of the hall. Their chance acquaintance, their guide, their odd pick-up, was standing there with his back to them, lighting a cigarette.

Gwen had stopped too. She came back to say in a low voice. "He's stopping in the hotel. He was at a table near the door. Very fluent in Italian." She moved away again and the man turned slowly.

"So you're staying here, too?" Mrs. Lawler said, calmly. "Can we give you some coffee as a reward for your help in the town?"

She implied, without exactly meaning it, that she and Mrs. Chilton were together.

"Thank you, but they brought me some at my table," he answered. "I'll watch you drinking yours, though."

And he walked off to where Gwen Chilton was waiting at the bar and presently came back with the girl, carrying both their cups to the small table in the lounge where Mrs. Lawler had established herself.

He was quite ready now to explain his own movements. A short stay on the French Riviera with some English friends, a long drive round the Corniche road to Genoa. Another long drive that day to Siena. Wonderful new roads, they all agreed.

"And where do you go now?" Mrs. Lawler asked. Mrs. Chilton did not seem particularly interested, but rather to have retired from the conversation into her usual self-pitying privacy.

"South," he answered. "Rome tomorrow and straight through to Naples."

"Not in one day?"

"Possibly. The autostradas are wonderful. I can rest when I get there: I'm going to friends. I'd rather not dawdle on the way."

"You must have a super car," Gwen said. She spoke suddenly, forcefully. Mrs. Lawler was startled, spilling her coffee spoon from the saucer to the floor. She noticed, as their unknown acquaintance dived politely after it that his hands, too, were shaking. Why? Or did they always shake? What did it matter, anyway?

The little, pointless episode did break up the party, though, Mrs. Chilton leaving first, as if disturbed by it. The man, who had only just regained his seat, rose once more when the girl got up and remained standing to take his own leave.

"You will be off before us in the morning," Mrs. Lawler said, looking up at him. "Though we are again due to start most uncomfortably early. So thank you again for your help over our sight-seeing, Mr. — er — "

"Owen Strong," he answered at once. "Thank you, Mrs. . . ."

"Rose Lawler."

"Mrs. Lawler."

They shook hands and as she was clearly about to leave herself, he helped her to her feet. Surprisingly strong in the wrist, she decided and no longer shaking. Not that it mattered, she told herself.

They exchanged a final good night and parted, Mrs.

Lawler making for the lifts, Mr. Strong for the front door.

Again she told herself, a little more regretfully than before, she had now seen the last of him.

Again she was wrong. Having undressed and turned out her top light, she pulled back her curtains and opened her window, deciding to risk the mosquitoes rather than suffocate. The lights of the town were still brilliant, stars shone in the sky, though there was no moon. Her window was three floors up at the back of the hotel. Directly below she looked down on a terrace with small tables and one or two figures seated at them with glasses or cups.

Owen Strong and Gwen Chilton were most noticeable. Also the courier, Billie and Mario, the coach driver. They sat at a table on the opposite side of the terrace to that of the other two.

"Well, well, well," Mrs. Lawler told herself, fastening up the window and pulling across half the curtain.

To shut out the mosquitoes? Certainly. And an unwelcome sight? A sad reminder? What nonsense!

Mrs. Lawler read a book for five minutes until the print began to swim, then put out her table lamp and slept.

17

Chapter II

The coach 'Roseanna' drew up outside the Siena hotel just after eight o'clock the next morning and three-quarters of an hour later the tour climbed sleepily on board, Billie counted them, Mario prepared to drive them away.

Mrs. Lawler, one of the first to leave the hotel, took her former place near the window, behind the driver: the Banks family did the same on the other side of the central aisle.

For a little while Mrs. Lawler hoped to see Mrs. Chilton arrive and take a seat farther back in the coach, but there was no sign of her.

"Did you see Mrs. Chilton at breakfast?" Billie asked her, tapping her biro against her front teeth.

No one had seen Mrs. Chilton at breakfast that morning, but Mario on being consulted, agreed that all the luggage belonging to this tour was on board. Every piece was there.

"Mrs. Chilton had no breakfast yesterday, so she told me," Mrs. Lawler said. "Perhaps she never does."

"She wouldn't be the first," Mrs. Franks said comfortably.

"They won't be told, neither," added Miss Hurry.

This seemed to close the question of Mrs. Chilton's food habits. Billie left the coach to look for her. The men lit cigarettes and pipes. After a further glance round her

18

Miss Banks also lit a cigarette, opening the window beside her to tip the ash out of it.

In five minutes Gwen Chilton appeared at the corner of the street, making for the hotel entrance, but not hurrying and not apparently recognising the coach 'Roseanna'. The other tourists stared but made no attempt to attract her attention. All except Mrs. Lawler, who called her name, but with no success.

However, Billie came out of the hotel just as Mrs. Chilton reached it, so with repeated apologies but no explanation the truant hurried up the steps of the coach and dropped into the seat beside Mrs. Lawler as Mario swung the coach away from the kerb.

"Late getting up again?" asked Mrs. Lawler, smiling.

"No. Early really."

"We didn't see you at breakfast."

"That! No, I went out. But the place didn't open till nine. Hopeless."

Guessing wildly but accurately, Mrs. Lawler said, "You wanted a bank?"

"How did you know?"

"I didn't. I guessed, because I wanted one myself yesterday and then realised we were leaving too early. But I was in time at San Gimignano. You should have gone there."

Mrs. Chilton said nothing.

"The trouble is," Mrs. Lawler went on, "we probably shan't get to Rome before they shut at twelve and you'll have to wait till they open again in the afternoon."

"Bloody hell," said Gwen Chilton softly.

Mrs. Lawler raised a disapproving eyebrow at her but said nothing. An unattractive, disagreeable girl; no wonder her husband had run out on her. No, that was wrong: she had left him.

The countryside flowed smoothly past, wide fields planted with rows of vines that climbed about, and were carried

19

by short sturdy trees. The vineyards alternated with crops of maize; corn for animals, not humans.

'Roseanna' swept on across the wide landscape. The hills were behind them now and after the excitement of the drives on the two previous days Mrs. Lawler found the view very restful, especially that part of it they saw from the autostrada where Mario displayed his driving talent to the full, giving way to strings of fast cars before pulling out to pass a group of slow lorries. She admired the road, with its strong central barrier decorated with a seemingly endless hedge of oleander bushes in many-coloured flower.

Her mind went back to the start of the tour. The easy flight, Billie's efficient care in getting them all together, the tunnels, the bridges, Pisa, San Gimignano ...

She sat up suddenly, for she had remembered some details of that fascinating mediaeval stone town that had escaped her when she reminded Mrs. Chilton of their stop there on their way to Siena.

She had visited the small bank to cash a traveller's cheque. Later she had gone back to the square before the cathedral to look about her for a suitable scene for a photograph. This was not easy because the tall stone towers that gave the little place both its distinction and its history, were too near and too high to make a complete picture. In the end she had taken the sunlit angle of the top of a steep side street and then re-crossing the square had gone back down the uneven cobbles towards the bank in that second square where there was a closed well much frequented by pigeons.

She had seen Mrs. Chilton leaving the bank. More than this she had seen Mrs. Chilton in the viewer of her camera. So she had a photograph of Mrs. Chilton on the current spool, leaving the bank in San Gimignano.

Mrs. Lawler glanced sideways at her companion. The girl was slumped in her seat, her head lolling against the back of it, eyes closed.

20

Looking about her as far as she was able Mrs. Lawler discovered that most of the travellers were dozing, the rest were occupied with maps, books, or in the case of Mrs. Banks, knitting. We left too early, she thought, we're all half asleep, with that small continental breakfast providing less than the right amount of energy. Why does Gwen want another bank today? Another bank . . . another breakfast . . . another coffee . . . She returned her gaze to the passing landscape but felt her eyelids droop. I'm as bad as the rest, she decided and smiled to herself because she knew there was no guilt attached to any one of them.

Billie roused her charges for a short coffee break at Ferrara. They stumbled sleepily out of the coach but revived quickly after hot drinks and sweet biscuits and in some cases slabs of the local cake called 'penforte' that they had bought in Siena the afternoon before.

Mrs. Lawler, who had secured some of this solid refreshment herself, pressed a slice upon Mrs. Chilton, but found the girl had managed to snatch a quick breakfast before they left Siena.

"Not at the hotel, surely?" Mrs. Lawler asked, astonished.

"No. Near the bank that wasn't open. That's why I was late back."

Mrs. Lawler thought this was most unlikely, but she could hardly refuse to believe it, though her memory of San Gimignano still nagged at her for explanation.

It nagged too at Mr. Banks, who in the privacy of his hotel room in Rome discussed it with his wife.

"Did you happen to hear that Mrs. Chilton, as she calls herself, on the coach?"

"I thought she was asleep most of the time."

"When she arrived late. To Billie as she came up the steps? And to Mrs. Lawler when she sat down?"

"No. We started with such a jerk I dropped my stitch and had quite a business picking it up again."

"You and your knitting! We shall be a laughing stock as usual!"

"What did the Chilton girl say, then?"

"That she'd tried to find a bank open to cash a traveller's cheque but hadn't found one."

"She might have known she wouldn't. It tells you about all that in the brochure."

"The point is," Mr. Banks went on impatiently, "she cashed one or got some money anyway, in that place we stopped at in the morning. Place with those bloody great towers."

"San Gimignano."

"That's right. I slipped in myself to be on the safe side and there she was, just finished making her signature. Didn't see me. Moved along towards the cashier with her handbag. First chap wanted to give her back her passport, waved it over the counter. I saw it."

He paused, looking at his wife. As usual she was knitting. She was always knitting, damn her. No point, really, taking her abroad, except they expected it at the office. Even more now he was managing director.

"I saw that passport," he said, so forcefully that Mrs. Banks looked up with a start. Reg always had to make a drama of every little thing he told you.

"I saw that passport," he repeated more gently, having secured her attention, "and it wasn't British and the name wasn't Chilton." ·

"He'd got hold of the wrong one, I suppose," said Mrs. Banks, returning to her work. She wished Reg would go down to the bar with his fairy tales, so she could do their unpacking. It would be worth hanging up her dresses and his suits because they would be in Rome for four nights.

"It wasn't the wrong one at all," said Mr. Banks. "Because she took it when the cashier gave it to her with the money. She was talking the lingo to him, too."

"Well, you talk Italian enough to get along," Mrs.

22

Banks assured him. She added, thoughtfully, "She got on the plane at Gatwick. I do remember that."

"Whoever said she didn't?" her husband snapped, sorry he had begun his strange story of their fellow-traveller. But he decided he had better keep it to himself if this was all the reception it got from Mildred.

So though he had a pleasant chat with Mrs. Lawler that evening over an apéritif before dinner he did not mention Mrs. Chilton's odd appearance in the bank at San Gimignano. When Gwen herself appeared and joined them he got to his feet but did not sit down again. He bought her a drink, then saying with very artificial heartiness that he must find his womenfolk, went away and did not appear again until all three of the Banks family took their places at the dinner table.

Mrs. Chilton had endured a very boring afternoon. They had reached Rome in time for lunch. After a short siesta Mrs. Lawler had come knocking at her door and without apology for disturbing her welcome rest had swept her out into the blistering sunshine. On foot they had tramped what seemed like miles to the Spanish Steps, where the schoolmistress had sat down and pointed out a bank on the other side of the road.

"We'll have a little rest here and then go on to the Piazza Venetia and see Capitol Square and laugh at the 'wedding cake' as I call it, the Victor Emmanuel white atrocity. Then we can find an ice or a coffee or something and get back here when the banks open at four."

All this they had done. The finish up at the bank had been the tricky part. But she had persuaded Mrs. Lawler to walk on slowly towards the hotel, saying she would catch her up and had then dashed into the bank before the nosy old bore could refuse. Inside the porch, out of sight, she had watched Mrs. Lawler hesitate, then walk away, while she made a play of searching in her bag, not finding what she sought, at last taking out a compact and lipstick, restoring her makeup and when she thought she had been

23

there long enough, moving back into the street and timing her movement so well that she caught up the school-mistress at the entrance to the hotel.

The following day was spent in very heavy sight-seeing, a renewal of delights for Mrs. Lawler at St. Peter's and the Vatican in the morning and in the afternoon a tour of well-known parts of ancient Rome and a drive through the Borghese Gardens, only spoiled by a sudden thunder-storm.

Mrs. Chilton endured it all, being quite uninterested in ancient Rome and quite untouched by works of genius in paint or marble or any other material. Her total indiffer-ence was matched by the stunned appreciation of the majority of the coach party and the open delight of a few, including Mrs. Lawler. The hired Italian guide who took Billie's place for the whole of this day and half the next found his customers very heavy on the hand, but dismissed them to himself as typical Britishers.

On the second full day in Rome the coach 'Roseanna' took its cargo of visitors outside the ancient city, travelling first of all past the Baths of Caracalla and along the Appian Way over the Roman pavement that in places seemed as good as when it was first laid.

On this drive, which took them to the hills again and past the Pope's summer palace of Castel Gandolfo, the tourists recovered to some extent from their prolonged immersion in Culture on the day before. They compared views on the trip so far, chiefly in respect of the food and comforts at the three hotels in Pisa, Siena and now Rome. They laughed about their difficulties with the language; they laughed even louder over the quaint appearance and habits of some of the natives, though they all agreed that the girls in the streets might have come from anywhere in England if you went by the clothes they wore.

"Or America or France for that matter," declared Mr. Woodruff, who had represented his firm on two brief occasions in New York and Paris.

24

"Probably did," Mrs. Blundells agreed. Her husband wasn't sticking up for himself against that jumped-up electronics boy with his showing-off. Besides, at home you only had to listen in the streets and you heard a right tower of Babel. Might be Brum or Sheffield. The Midlands. That was where the foreigners came for ideas, saleable ideas. Why, they got them in the shop most days of the week. Retail hardware and she didn't care who knew it.

In her front seat with Mrs. Chilton at her side as before Mrs. Lawler read her guide book after they left the Appian Way. She had taken a melancholy pleasure in that long, straight graveyard as they bumped along it, but had not wanted to get down to take photographs when 'Roseanna' stopped for that purpose. Nor had Mrs. Chilton shown any wish to get out. Nor Mrs. Banks, knitting away by the window on the opposite side of the coach; nor Penny Banks, smoking her endless chain of cigarettes with the window beside her pulled halfway down.

A horrid girl Penny, Mrs. Lawler had now decided. Uncouth, grubby, dressed in near rags, she had been unattractive hitherto but an object more for pity than wrath. This morning, however, she had shown herself as dangerous as an adder in the grass, as pointlessly aggressive if in any way disturbed.

Moving towards the coach that morning, Penny had pushed past her mother who was in polite competition with Mrs. Lawler to let the other climb up first. She had been about to push past the latter also, but Mrs. Lawler had put out an arm to stop her, saying mildly, "Your mother first, surely, Miss Banks." Whereupon Miss Banks had lifted a heavy-sandalled foot and kicked out at Mrs. Lawler's shin.

The schoolmistress had not spent years with the young in vain. Nor had she lost all of her very highly trained physical skill. She jumped quickly up two steps as the girl's foot came at her, so that Penny, instead of instant revenge, met an instant steel punishment far more severe than Mrs. Lawler's rebuke. She fell back against her father screaming obscene abuse in rage and pain.

Mrs. Lawler simply went on up the steps, followed by Mrs. Banks. Neither said anything. Mr. Banks gripped his daughter, told her to shut her filthy trap and threw her up the steps where Mario, eyes shining with excited amusement, for he had not fully understood what had happened, had left the driver's seat when the two older women had moved to their places.

Penny Banks, writhing at the top of the steps, hit out at the nearest thing to her, which was Mario's face bending down to see what had happened. The next instant she was picked up and swung round into the place behind her mother. Two very large hands held her down for a few seconds, then released her. Billie's voice said, with professional calm. "Is anything the matter, Miss Banks? Your father thinks..."

"Bugger my father!" yelled Miss Banks, but her foot hurt, Mario was back in the driver's seat, neither her mother nor Mrs. Lawler was looking at her, the other people in the coach, after a few nervous laughs, were taking no notice. She collapsed into tears. But Mario had started the engine, so this final bid for importance attracted no attention whatever.

All the same when 'Roseanna' stopped at a viewpoint above the volcanic lake, looking back across the blue water at Castel Gandolfo on the opposite height, Mrs. Lawler said to her companion, "I should like to take a photograph here."

Mrs. Chilton prepared to leave her seat. Mrs. Lawler went on, "Will you come with me? I see that nasty child has followed the Bankses out. You could guard me from her while I'm concentrating on a picture."

She spoke in a deliberately light-hearted manner, but her inner fear was quite genuine. Unbelievable it might be, but real violence could not be ruled out, nor a real weapon.

So Mrs. Chilton went first and Mrs. Lawler followed,

camera in hand. The rest of the tourists were spread along the low wall at the edge of the lay-by. Penny Banks was sitting on the wall, her injured foot supported upon the opposite knee, showing it to Billie, who had a small First-Aid box open, offering the girl its contents.

"Safe enough for the moment," said Mrs. Lawler happily over her shoulder, turning back at once to focus her camera upon the distant summer palace.

But there was no answer and when she had finished and turned round she saw that Mrs. Chilton had walked away to the edge of the road and was staring down it where it wound away from the lake and back to the plain below the hills.

'Roseanna' took them all into Frascati at mid-morning for coffee and then back to Rome for lunch at the hotel. There was no further trouble with the Banks family. Covered by an ample dressing the injured foot did not seem to be much damaged.

"Bashed the big toe to judge by the blood," young Woodruff said with authority. "Stubbed it on the steps, didn't she?"

No one wanted to discuss it with him. Bleeding from stubbed toes was not a favourite topic. Miss Banks climbed the steps after her mother, given a push from behind by her father and a pull from a grinning Mario in front. But there were no more hysterics.

At lunch, to Mrs. Lawler's relief, two more women joined the table she was sharing with Gwen Chilton. They explained themselves in pleasant gentle voices; Myra Donald, a widow, Florence Jeans, unmarried. Both in the Civil Service, working at Lytham St. Annes, Lancashire. Both reasonably experienced travellers and they shared Mrs. Lawler's interest in the arts. They suggested some more sight-seeing on foot that afternoon, but Mrs. Lawler had had enough for the day, she told them. In fact her encounter with Penny Banks had alarmed and shaken her more than she was prepared to acknowledge and though

27

she now knew she need not in future lack real companions on this tour, she was tired and she wanted to rest and write a few letters. They would meet at dinner, she told her new friends.

Mrs. Chilton had left the dining table earlier than the other three. She had joined in their conversation, Mrs. Lawler had noted, without effort, but with no eagerness. She looked as pale as ever and ate very little. She must be ill, the schoolmistress thought.

Between five and six o'clock Mrs. Lawler decided to go out, buy stamps and post her letters and after that make her way to the square nearest to her hotel and order an ice at the big open-air restaurant there.

The late afternoon sun was very hot, the tables and chairs spread in a cool shade. Mrs. Lawler, with a thin air-mailed copy of an English newspaper in her hand, the first she had seen since leaving Gatwick, began to read as she waited for her ice. When it arrived she put the paper down and began to eat. The ice was delicious, the air clear and remarkably free from petrol fumes, the milling crowds colourful, happy, charming, better dressed, better mannered than in the deplorable Piccadilly Circus of recent times. This was excellent, this was wholly excellent, this was what she had . . .

At the other side of the spread of chairs and tables, sitting close together at a table far out into the street, she saw Gwen Chilton and the scar-faced guide of Siena . . . Strong, wasn't it . . . Yes, Owen Strong.

Chapter III

"SHE'S SEEN US," Owen said to Gwen, "but don't look about to find her. We don't want her coming over."

"Why not?"

"Too nosy. Too sharp. She frightens me."

"Get on with you."

He gave her the comic smile and patted her knee under the table. Gwen smiled back.

"Besides," Owen went on, "you haven't told me half that sad story of yours."

Gwen fumbled in her handbag for her handkerchief and dabbed at her eyes. But to her annoyance and alarm the tears refused to flow. She tried to sob but it did not sound very convincing.

"Go ahead," Owen said calmly, disregarding these efforts. "Or would you rather I waved to Mrs. Lawler?"

"You dare!" Gwen sat up straight in genuine alarm. "Besides," she added waspishly, "she's heard the lot. All eleven years of it."

"I bet she hasn't. No, don't tell me. Just get on with the last six, was it? After you discovered about the girl in Croydon."

"I told him I had enough evidence to divorce him and had a very good mind to do it."

"Why didn't you?"

"I wasn't sure his business wasn't cracking. I wasn't

29

going to be left with nothing. And her to have what there was."

Owen smiled again.

"Did you tell that sensible decision to Mrs. Highbrow Lawler?"

"What d'*you* think?"

"You wouldn't like it if I did."

Owen's face was still pleasantly comic, but his voice held a cutting note that stopped Gwen's breath. He glanced at her, but waited patiently. He was in no immediate hurry.

At last she said, changing the subject, "I thought you said you were going to Naples?"

"I did. And I was."

"To stay with friends."

"Yes."

"Then why are you back?"

"The visit was over. I wanted to come back. Don't say why to Rome. You know I came back to find *you*."

She wanted desperately to believe it. If it was genuine he could find a way for her from the position she was in through no fault of her own. The tour was all right. But at the end of it? She had a vision of arriving back at Gatwick. Who would she find there to welcome her? Him — or —

She shivered violently and one or two people at neighbouring tables looked at her curiously. Owen, who noticed everything, whose eyes had never stopped recording their whole surrounding scene, waved to the white-coated elderly waiter to ask for their bill.

"She's still there," he said, meaning Mrs. Lawler. "We'll go to my hotel. But we'll walk down to the Spanish Steps to throw her off the scent."

"How?" asked Gwen sulkily. "She won't follow us there, will she?"

"I think not," he answered in a grave, wholly natural voice. "It wouldn't occur to her."

30

"Well, then?"

But the bill had arrived and Owen was paying it and chatting affably with the waiter, so she got no answer, though she gave herself the satisfaction of locating Mrs. Lawler and waving to her. Owen Strong might be taking her to his hotel and she had no doubt of his intention in so doing. In fact she would have felt insulted if she proved to be wrong. But he wasn't going to have the last word and he wasn't going to screw any more of the past out of her.

At Owen's hotel he collected the key of his room while she sat with a drink in the lounge. They went quietly up together and she was not at all wrong about his intention. But very wrong about that last word.

She lay watching him dress, pleasantly drowsy and very contented. She had enjoyed herself more than she had expected and far more than she had thought possible when she joined the coach at Genoa. Not a single one of the men on their plane who looked even capable had turned up on 'Roseanna'. The thought of two whole dreary weeks with that lot . . .

Owen looked round at her. Nicely relaxed, ready to give the facts he wanted. Just a little shake and she'd fall like a ripe plum — well, not exactly a plum, a bit shrivelled, even if ripe.

He stopped drooling to himself and leaving his jacket hanging on a chair went over and sat on the side of the bed and picking up Gwen's left hand gently slid the wedding ring off and stared at the bare finger.

"How long did you say you've been married?"

"Eleven years," she answered, "and each of them after the first, a lifetime . . ."

"Of misery," Owen finished for her. "Then how come the ring has left no impression whatever."

A familiar warning bell sounded in Gwen's brain.

"The ring?" she repeated to gain time, to choose which tale would go down best.

"Yes, the wedding ring. I don't believe you, Gwen, my

31

darling. I don't believe you've worn this ring for eleven years."

He was making it too easy, but still she was puzzled. He had accused her so pleasantly, so smoothly. He was no jealous boy trying to work up his passion by rootling in her past. Oh no. He was far older than she was, in more ways than one. So what was his game? Better cut it off short, but stop the questions first.

Snatching her ring back from him, ramming it on to her finger, she wriggled away to the opposite side of the bed, swung her legs to the floor and said with a well-simulated choking sob, "All right, I haven't worn it all that time." And defiantly, "I always take it off at night, anyhow."

Owen laughed aloud. Gwen went across the room in one bound to smack his crooked face but he caught the hand in such a fierce grip that she screamed, though no sound came, for his other hand covered her mouth.

She was not frightened for she knew he had not lost his temper and he was the kind of man who did not become dangerous until his temper ruled him. So she let herself go limp and found herself plunged on the bed again, while Owen walked across to the wash basin to clean his hand of her saliva.

"Get dressed, you silly bitch," he said in his gentle voice.

Gwen wept a few genuine tears.

Later, restoring her hair and make-up, she told him the second version of her marital troubles. She did it well.

"I didn't want you to know," she began. "Roy Chilton has been my boss for eleven years. He was married all that time, five years before, actually. At first I thought he'd get a divorce, but then as it went on and on . . ."

"You realised he did not intend to give up his family?"

"That's right. I know it's an old story, but it does happen. In the end . . ."

"You ran out on him?"

32

She nodded and he let her finish the work on her face. Then he said, "What are you using for money?"

She was not caught. In fact she was relieved. Money. That was what he wanted from her, was it? Poor nit. She'd begun to think he was dangerous. But no, not at all. Just over-confident.

She looked round at him and saw with a slight inner chill that he had taken her handbag and had opened it. But it was not money he was after. He rummaged quickly, turning things about roughly, much to her indignation. Finally he pulled out, not her wallet, but her passport, saying with an air of triumph, "So now perhaps you'll tell me. What were you doing in Switzerland three weeks ago, was it? This'll tell me the actual dates, won't it?"

Got him again, she thought, waiting, her face very pale but wary.

He dropped her bag on the bed, she pounced and secured it and began to tidy the ruffled contents, bending her head over it to hide the smile she could not help widening her mouth. But she saw in the long mirror on the wardrobe his blank astonishment and confusion.

For, instead of the foreign document he expected to find inside the British cover, he held a genuine English passport, in the name of Gwendoline Chilton, with the usual unflattering photograph, quite unmistakably herself. And there was no evidence on any page to show she had visited Switzerland that year or any other year during the lifetime of that passport. The most recent entry marked her arrival in Italy, at Genoa, five days ago.

Gwen looked up at him. Rage and disappointment but no regret for his shockingly ill-mannered behaviour. So she said quietly, not wishing to goad him into any further physical attack, "If you've quite finished with my passport can I have it back, please, and I'll be on my way."

He threw it in her direction, but she caught it and pushing it down into her handbag got to her feet and moved towards the door of the room. He did nothing to prevent her. But before she opened the door he said, "I want to know what you were doing in Switzerland last month. Some day you will tell me."

That stopped her. She turned about, standing very close to the door as if for support.

"I was never in Switzerland. You've looked at my passport, you bloody insolent devil! You know I wasn't!"

"You were. In another name, I reckon . . . another passport. You'll not get away with that game for long!"

"Liar! I was never there. Why d'you keep saying it? What do you want to know for? You can't prove I was. Can you? Can you?"

"Oh yes. I can. Because I saw you in Geneva. Twice."

That really shook her, but she rallied. He had given himself away, now. She turned and opened the door, holding the knob ready to slam after her.

"You saw me, did you? I thought you were staying with friends on the Riviera? So what were *you* doing in Geneva?"

She was out of the room and away before the stream of whispered vicious curses had begun to pour from his crooked mouth.

At the hotel Mrs. Lawler sat with her two new friends in the lounge. sipping a long crimson drink they had recommended. She was not enjoying it much.

"Too like a powerful cough mixture," she said. "But nice and cold."

"You'd prefer sherry?" Mrs. Donald said.

"So would you, really, Myra," her friend, Miss Jeans told her.

"You were telling us about Mrs. Chilton," Mrs. Donald said, disregarding Florence.

"So I was." Mrs. Lawler leaned forward. "But she's just come in. I think she may join us. No, it's all right, she's making for the lifts. Yes, well, what was I saying?

34

The stranger in Siena. I don't really think they'd met before. But one can't know that."

"She may have attracted him. She's rather attractive in a wispy sort of way."

"Yes," said Mrs. Lawler. Mrs. Chilton had not struck her as being attractive in any sort of way. She had flattered herself that Mr. Strong had joined them at coffee on her own account, to exchange a little interesting conversation. She could not recollect Mrs. Chilton contributing anything at all on that occasion and very little except her melancholy personal history on any other. Now that she herself had found two companions with whom she could discuss and compare the antiquities and the arts, she thought she would prefer to drop Mrs. Chilton, except for that seat on the coach she could hardly warn her away from.

But Mrs. Chilton, who had also welcomed the inclusion of the two Civil Service ladies at her table, for a very different reason from Mrs. Lawler's, arrived in good time to join the three as a matter of course, and even took it upon herself to suggest sharing a bottle of Chianti to drink with the meal, a habit she established for several days, rather to their tolerant amusement.

Myra and Flo, as they wished to be called, were not slow to work towards an open question about the mysterious Mr. Strong. They did this through Mrs. Lawler, now Rose to them.

"I thought you told us, Rose, he was driving on to Naples," Myra said.

"That's what he told Gwen and me," she answered, and turning to the girl, who had not offered any addition to the talk after Flo had mentioned Owen, she asked, "Perhaps you know where he's been?"

"Owen Strong? Why should I? He said Naples, yes, I remember that. Three days ago in Siena, wasn't it?"

"I suppose he's on his way back. He didn't tell you?"

"Why should he?"

They were all looking at her. Proper set of vultures.

But for want of a better story she told them the truth.

"He didn't say and I didn't ask him, actually. You see," she went on, trying to tell them nothing and yet satisfy the curiosity she saw in their three pairs of eyes, "we just met up by accident in that big square with the fountains and four big statues round it. I was taking some pictures and he just came up to me, like he did in Siena and said, 'Hullo, still sight-seeing?' So I said 'Yes' and he said, 'Come and have an ice' so we walked along to the Popolo and that's where you saw me, Mrs. Lawler."

The others nodded. If he hadn't said what he was doing in Rome there was no object in pressing questions upon Gwen Chilton. Even Mrs. Lawler asked no more. Besides, what was the point? If the man was on his way back up the length of Italy well, so were they. Only making now towards Florence before crossing the mountains to the shores of the Adriatic. If he was not going to Florence, if he purposed to use the autostrada all the way north they would not see him again. This was probably the more desirable from Gwen's point of view. She clearly took no real interest in the man. Why should she unless on the rebound from her husband's callous behaviour. But curiosity prompted one last question.

"Where did you throw him off this evening?" Rose asked gaily, with a side look at her new friends.

Gwen smiled.

"Outside his hotel. He asked me in for a drink, but it was getting late and I wanted to have plenty of time to change for dinner."

It had not been late when the pair left their table, Rose remembered. And Gwen had not come in early; in fact only just in reasonable time. What a liar the girl was, she reflected.

This opinion was only confirmed later that evening. She left the two Civil Servants directly after she had finished her coffee and went to her room to try to learn some Italian. She admired the sound of the language, but found

36

it very difficult to imitate. With the help of French and a little Latin remembered from her own school days, she could read the simple Italian of her phrase book without looking at the English translation. But speaking it was another matter.

She had struggled with the problem for about half an hour when a gentle knock at her door brought her to her feet. She dropped the phrase book on her bed as she passed it. Gwen Chilton stood outside, nervous, apologetic.

"May I come in?" she asked.

Mrs. Lawler was not enthusiastic and showed it. But her manners held up and she welcomed the visitor with adequate politeness.

Gwen waited to be offered a seat. There were only two; the armchair that Mrs. Lawler had left and a straight-backed small one, covered with Mrs. Lawler's cast off clothes from earlier in the day. So the visitor got the armchair and Mrs. Lawler sat down on the bed.

"Yes?" she asked, in much the same way she had been used in the past to receive complaints, confidences, plans, troubles, criticisms, pleadings, from the girls with whom she worked.

It was not a helpful start to any conversation, not meant to be. But it was a test of genuine need and proved as effective as ever.

"You must be fed up with my moanings," Gwen said carefully. Her opinion of Mrs. Lawler was changing and she spoke with conviction, surprising even herself.

"They say confession is always good for the soul," replied Mrs. Lawler, thus adding to Gwen's confusion.

"Well, you'd better have it straight out," she said, deciding a direct line was needed if it was to help her at all. "The thing is Owen — Mr. Strong — got me to join him for a drink at his hotel and tried to — well — to date me. I'm scared of him."

"Is *that* all?" said Mrs. Lawler calmly. "Surely not."

The old cow was really the limit! Gwen flushed angrily,

pulled herself together with an effort and tried, not very successfully, to produce tears.

"Now don't begin to cry again," Mrs. Lawler said, not unkindly but with a weary attempt to cut out an unnecessary interlude. "I begin to think you must have been on the stage or studied for it sometime."

The fact that this was true did nothing to restore Mrs. Chilton. She wiped her eyes, blew her nose, sat up straight and challenged Mrs. Lawler.

"You don't believe me! You think I'm lying to you!"

"Not for the first time. No, don't interrupt me. Do you think over thirty years of dealing with the female young — including my former self — haven't taught me to spot a congenital liar? I'm not insulting you. You are insulting me by imagining you can put it across me."

Gwen had never in her life been spoken to in quite this way before. She had enjoyed shouting matches with her early teachers, when her fluency had gained her both support and applause from her classmates. She had worked herself into drama groups by means of this same facility, and from there to auditions and agents and a brief period in a school of acting. But there was no real talent, no sticking power . . .

She rallied quickly. She said, attempting hurt dignity and very nearly succeeding, "When have I lied to you?"

"That's better," said Mrs. Lawler, recognising the end of fantasy, at least for the moment. "When you told me you must get to a bank, after they'd closed, because you had no Italian currency. Actually you cashed a traveller's cheque or something at San Gimignano. I saw you coming out when I was looking at that old well. And Mr. Banks told me only today that he was in the bank at San Gimignano when you were there. Didn't you notice him? He recognised you."

No. She had not noticed him. She had been too damned scared, using that Swiss passport. But it had worked like a dream. After all, why shouldn't it?

38

As Gwen made no answer Mrs. Lawler, to goad her into fresh truth, said gently, "Did you hope I'd offer to lend you Italian notes to tide you over? As I did, of course. And then forget to settle up? Why else pretend? Did you cash some more here in Rome? But you still haven't settled, have you?"

This was getting far too near the bone, Gwen decided. And real nasty, too. Well, she'd shame her wicked suggestion, anyhow.

Pulling her handbag open Mrs. Chilton dragged out her wallet, tore from it several dirty five hundred lire notes and showered them upon Mrs. Lawler where she still sat, upright in judgment and self-righteousness, upon the bed.

"I *did* forget!" she swore a hair-raising oath to confirm it. "Take your filthy money. I wish I'd never accepted it!"

"This is far too much," Mrs. Lawler said, not at all disturbed by the all-too familiar tantrums. "Here, take these back. You haven't finished telling me the real truth about Mr. Strong."

"As if you cared!" Gwen managed a very realistic sob.

"Nonsense," Mrs. Lawler said, with splendid impartiality.

So Mrs. Chilton expressed her fears of their casual acquaintance rather more clearly and Mrs. Lawler listened and wondered more and more deeply why exactly the girl was doing it.

But in the end all she could find to say was, "My dear Gwen, you have only to keep with the rest of us. Refuse to be alone with him. Refuse any sort of invitation he makes. I had my doubts of him myself. But not this sort of thing at all."

"What then?" Gwen asked, feeling another slight chill.

"Never mind," answered Mrs. Lawler. "In any case we have only one more day in Rome. After that we go to Florence. You don't suppose he's likely to follow us there, do you?"

"I wouldn't put it past him," Mrs. Chilton said gloomily.

39

Chapter IV

WHEN OWEN STRONG recovered his temper after Gwen
left him, he brushed his thinning hair, put on his tie and
then his jacket and went down to the bar where he ordered
an apricot drink and went to the telephone while it was
being prepared to speak to a friend he addressed as Rollo.

He lingered over his drink which he took to a small
table near the hotel entrance. The friend had not far to
come to the hotel, but for Owen the time dragged until
he appeared.

Rollo was small, middle-aged, shabbily dressed. He followed Owen into the dining room when it opened for the
evening meal and ate heartily while the former did all
the talking. Then, back in the lounge, Owen, sipping at
first coffee, later a succession of brandies, the explanations
were succeeded by orders.

Owen's Italian was good and though, seeing most of
the hotel visitors were natives, he had to keep his voice
low, his companion had no difficulty in taking Mr. Strong's
instructions. The Ambrosia Hotel, the tour coach 'Roseanna'. Its route and time table and report back in an hour.

"Si, signore. Prestissimo."

Rollo knew the Ambrosia. As a freelance journalist,
far freer these days than he cared for, he prided himself on
knowing all the Roman hotels and at least one member of
the staff in each. In the bigger, the more opulent, this

40

might be only the commissionaire who guarded the front entrance against his attempted invasion. More usually it was one of the kitchen underlings who could be bribed for a pitifully small handful of lire.

As now. The big coach was garaged in the next street. It was being cleaned probably, unless Mario the driver was still tinkering with the engine.

Rollo found two men at work on 'Roseanna'. One, the big one in overalls, spanner in hand, other tools on the ground beside him, was leaning into the depths of the engine. The other, a thin boy in jeans and a filthy tee-shirt, was sweeping rubbish along the central aisle of the coach, pausing every now and then to pick up some piece more solid than the rest.

"Here! I'll have that," Rollo said with a laugh holding out his hand.

"Anything I find I keep," the boy said. He was holding a glossy looking production that Rollo recognised as the brochure put out by the company that ran these particular tours. "So long as it don't have the owner's name on it."

"Well, has it?"

"No. So it's mine."

"What'll you take for it?"

"I'd like to look at it. After that I might sell."

"I'll give you twenty lire."

The boy put the brochure on a seat beyond Rollo's reach and turned away, whistling a pop tune well known in all western Europe.

Rollo, with a glance now and then at Mario, who showed signs of coming to the end of his engine inspection, gradually increased his offer while the boy slowly swept out the rest of the coach, taking the final heap of rubbish into a plastic bag he held at the top of the rear steps. The brochure had travelled beside him on the seats, the price had remained unfixed but had been slowly swelling.

It was Mario who resolved the matter. He brought his body upright, he shut down the engine cover, he wiped his great hands on an oily rag that dangled from a pocket of his overalls. He walked down the length of the coach just as the boy finished disposing of his pile of rubbish. Mario leaned in over the boy's shoulder to pick up the brochure.

"I would like to have that, seeing it's been discarded," Rollo said.

Mario turned it over. Certainly, it was unnamed.

"He says he owns any useful rubbish," Rollo went on. "I offered to pay him for it."

"How much?" asked Mario.

Rollo told him the whole process of the bargaining.

"Give him ten lire," ordered Mario, handing the brochure to its new owner. The boy accepted the small final sum, stamped his foot, emptied his plastic bag over Rollo's feet and shouldered his broom with a defiant gesture, tears running down his smooth brown cheeks.

Mario burst into loud laughter. Rollo, shaking off the rubbish from his shoes, rolled up the plastic bag and slung it after the boy. It fell several yards short of him and he paid no notice, but walked on with bowed head, still suffering from his double failure.

"You go on again tomorrow?" Rollo asked as Mario turned away.

"Day after. You can look it up in that book. Want to join us? We've several empty places. All Inglese, though."

He made a face of disgust, at which Rollo smiled.

"No young ones?"

"A little junkie with idiot parents. A so-called widow, good-looker, but hysterical."

"That all?"

"Bourgeois wives and dried-up spinsters. Bah!"

He spat into the pile of rubbish. Rollo decided it was time to move away. He had done better than he expected and Signor Strong was not a patient man, though he paid well for his occasional small assignments.

Owen was delighted to have the brochure; it was going

to save him a lot of boring and perhaps rather dangerous work and a lot of time keeping tabs on this elusive project, this question of Gwen, calling herself Mrs. Chilton.

He paid Rollo handsomely but got rid of him at once, with the usual warning to keep his mouth shut under pain of extreme penalties. The little journalist grinned knowingly as he took his leave, but he did not underrate the threat. There had been a fellow journalist who had gossipped about Signor Strong's activities and had not been seen in Rome again. He had been found several months later in a smashed car at the foot of those high cliffs on the coast road between Sorrento and Amalfi. Rollo liked money; he seldom had enough for his careful needs. He was quite uninterested in his employer's business. Secrecy was no effort, especially as it seemed to guarantee further employment, whereas the opposite, besides bringing retribution from Strong might also bring danger from the police.

When Rollo had gone Owen turned his mind to his next problem. How much of what Gwen had told him, sitting in the pleasant shade at the café in the Plaza dei Populo was true, half true, or altogether false? She had lied about her relationship with that boss of hers. Not a husband, perhaps a lover, perhaps indeed a boss, but what kind of boss? Perhaps he should have got into contact with her in Geneva when he had seen her going into one of the banks with which he was very familiar. She had been nervous, but controlled. She had been carrying a large suitcase. She had kept him waiting a full hour, tinkering first with the engine of his car, then reading a Swiss newspaper, lounging behind the wheel. He had been dressed as a chauffeur and he had managed to slip into a convenient and legitimate parking place. But a whole hour! ... No wonder he had been half asleep when she came out at last, carrying the suitcase that now looked suspiciously light from the way it swung in her hand.

He was too slow. He had moved at last, had crossed the road where she had crossed. Was just behind her as she stopped a cruising taxi. But he heard her direction to the driver given in French. "To the airport — drive fast — a plane to catch for England. But first to the Universal for my luggage."

So, he had decided, he had lost out on that one. But after a day or two, playing his usual game, he had pulled off a useful move on the French Riviera and afterwards, making for Naples, had stopped at Genoa to visit the airport there. Purely on spec. These hordes of tourists. Sometimes, among them . . .

Well, there it was. Gwen, easily remembered, with a tall, lean, elderly Englishwoman, country type, perhaps even county; do-gooder, perhaps. Hardly that, too intelligent, his cynical mind suggested. But anyway, Gwen as he now called her, with the same anxious face she had worn in Geneva a fortnight before. Quite unmistakable.

So now what? In Switzerland he had decided she was a frightened, obedient doll, not quite in her first youth, but pretty enough when she smiled, as he discovered later; arranging to cache the large sum she carried in that heavy suitcase and then go straight back home, having filled up that empty case with some of her belongings waiting at the hotel.

Then what was she doing in Italy, going quietly on a tour of the three important cities? Rome, Florence, Venice, the brochure told him. Why? And why the give-away wedding ring? Not that it mattered. Particularly if she was, after all, just a common whore.

But she was not that, he decided. She was experienced, she was skilful, she was what they called "a good lay", or used to call it. Owen shivered a little as he accused himself of being perhaps out of date, behind the times, reaching the moment when he must retire from his lucrative career or business as it might better be called. And yet he was not in a position to do so. Had he ever been? Had he not always been catching up on his losses, all his life? If he gave up now, how would he spend his time, how provide for his permanently expensive tastes?

Owen drowned these morbid thoughts in another brandy taken from his personal supply in his room. Afterwards he decided to continue his pursuit of Gwen until he discovered what she was really at. He decided he was interested in her personally as well, quite apart from the business angle. She was not afraid of him, for one thing. All that guff about a hopeless affair with her boss was sheer balls and she had understood that he knew it. But she had not been afraid, for she had rounded on him before she walked out. What was he doing in Switzerland? No denial of her appearance there, but a definite counter-threat. Great girl — perhaps. He'd damn well find out.

On their last day in Rome the 'Roseanna' tourists were to visit the catacombs in the morning and the Colosseum in the afternoon. Having avoided the evening tours of the two previous nights Mrs. Lawler decided to go on both of these expeditions.

Besides, there was Gwen, appealing to her to be there.

"You aren't still nervous about that man?" she asked the girl, as they waited to take their places in the coach the next morning.

"I am, you know," Gwen answered, though she looked really pretty that morning, Rose Lawler thought. She was wearing a fresh sleeveless cotton dress or rather shift, about mid-thigh in length, but the legs were good and could take it. Far better than some of the other women, who looked well enough in slacks but not so good when they disclosed wide expanses of solid flesh or spindly blue-veined shanks.

Penny Banks dragged up the coach steps in another multi-coloured ankle length piece of material, topped by her usual dirty off-white sweater. But she stood aside for her mother to climb the steps before her and Mrs. Lawler, with a cheerful "Thank you, Penny; what a lovely day" plunged quickly behind Mrs. Banks and received nothing in return but a fierce look and a movement of the mouth that might produce a collection of spit or merely a protruded tongue.

"You've got that girl taped," Gwen said as they drove away. "She didn't do a thing when you cut in getting on board. Just looked daggers. And she hasn't even started up one of those cigarettes. Pot, aren't they?"

"So that's what the smell is?" Rose answered, taking it for granted Gwen knew or she would not have suggested it. She merely turned to glance at Penny, before removing her gaze and smile to her Civil Service friends, three rows behind on the girl's side.

It was indeed a lovely day, a hot sun in a clear sky, still blue at that fairly early hour. It seemed a pity to be going to spend precious time underground, in corridors haunted by ancient fear and death, persecution and faith, the obstinacy of political power and the answering power of religion, which were perhaps aspects of the same thing. How often had they not discussed these matters in her college days and later listened to recurring arguments at the schools where she had taught? She looked forward to renewing such talk with Myra and Flo that evening. Useless to start it with Gwen now. The girl had already declared that her interest in the catacombs was identical with that of most of the coach load; anticipation of getting a "gowlish" or "goolish" thrill from the display of bones, skulls and other relics.

The little garden beside the catacombs' public entrance was bereft of the flowers she remembered from her earlier visit to Rome, which had been in April. But the grass patch had been watered and there were leaves on the trees. Mrs. Lawler suddenly felt that she could not bear to go underground. She moved back to her own queue to tell Gwen, who protested strongly that she needed to have a hand to cling to.

"Mrs. Donald or Miss Jeans here will do that," Rose

said, laughing as the two others moved forward, hearing their names spoken. "I shall stay up here. I've been before, you know. These two know much more about it than I ever did."

"May I really hold on to you?" Gwen asked them. "I didn't think Rose would desert me."

"Of course," they answered and Myra Donald at once took one of Gwen's hands to pull her forward, for their queue was moving on, urged by the Italian guard at the entrance.

Mrs. Lawler returned to the garden and sat down in the shade of trees to enjoy the blissful air, the scent of water-sprinkled grass, the view of wide fields still free of the Rome that had encroached so rapidly since her first visit. She took off her dark glasses to look at the now whitening Mediterranean sky and the brilliant patches of sunlight on the road and beyond.

She put them on again suddenly as a long black car slid to a stop behind 'Roseanna'. She was sitting with her back turned to the entrance when Owen Strong walked up, took a ticket and was allowed to proceed inside to join the tail of the still waiting queue —

Well, well, well, thought Mrs. Lawler. So Gwen was right, after all, not exaggerating. She was glad she had not gone in. Gladder still she had put the girl in charge of her competent friends. She looked forward to hearing the outcome.

But she was disappointed. Mr. Strong came out again well ahead of the 'Roseanna' tour, got into his car without looking round at all and drove off. Gwen came out chatting and laughing with Myra and Flo. She did not say a single word about Owen Strong either on the way back to the hotel or after they got there.

But she joined the Civil Servants and Rose Lawler at lunch, making up a quartette that gathered as a matter of course from that time onward. They were all together at the Colosseum the same afternoon, dodging in and out of the many other tours and the hordes of mixed local citizens and private sight-seers, clambering up the wide steep stairs of this ancient place of entertainment, terror and death.

Mrs. Lawler leaned on the parapet of the terrace where their guide had gathered them together to explain the wonders of the building and its history. As before, ten years before, when she had come there privately with a friend, Rose deplored the absence of the arena floor. It was interesting to see exposed that multitude of little rooms and dens where fighting men, destined victims, wild animals and their keepers had been kept until their time came to go up to fight for their lives or suffer against impossible odds. But the general effect was muddled, presenting none of the imperial grandeur the wide sweeping floor space of the arena would have presented.

She was shocked too by the gross decay she found all over the terraces. She remembered rows of intact seats that were now heaps of rubble. She remembered too Henry James's story of an American girl sitting with her boy friend on one of these seats thinking about their history, their former use. Now, seemingly, with scaffolding all about the vast ruin, its total collapse was threatened. Crowds still flooded up the public entrance stairs, but used only one, the only safe one, now.

She heard her name called and turned to go. No point in taking another photograph. Her ten-year-old pictures showed far more antiquity, far less crumbling featureless stone.

She found she was separated from Myra and Flo by an alien group that divided them from her, but she made no attempt to push past, deciding without rancour that they would meet easily when the 'Roseanna' tour gathered again about the guide's raised and waving arm.

But at the top of the wide stairs there was a parting of the ways. The alien group, hesitating, sub-dividing, split into a disorganised mob, some pushing forward, some, but

48

only a few, beginning to go down. While Mrs. Lawler hesitated she felt a smart push in the back that propelled her forward, missed a step, knew she was falling, grasped that she was on the staircase and with a determined, conscious effort, began her rapid descent.

As Myra told her afterwards, "Flo and I were at the bottom looking back to see if you were coming. We saw you stumble and were horrified."

Flo took up the tale. "It was like a slalom at first. You were dodging to right and left, two steps at a time, upright, steady as a rock . . ."

"People flabbergasted, struck still to keep out of your way . . ."

"So you had a very narrow but clear run to the bottom. Then the roar of applause . . ."

"And anger! Some people were shaking their fists," Myra reminded her. "Why did you do it, Rose?"

But Mrs. Lawler only said, "Thank God I changed into slacks after lunch. Where are the others?"

They were beginning to tell her when the guide came up to them, white-faced, trembling, chiefly with fury, partly with concern. Mad Englishwomen! He had suffered from their appalling eccentricities before, but never quite like this!

"Signora, signora!" he spluttered, his English drowned in unspoken Italian curses.

"I'm sorry," Mrs. Lawler said in his own language. "I was falling and with all those people on the stairs I might have been killed and taken a lot of others with me."

She spoke carefully, understandably, but with a bad English accent and much hesitation. The guide found it impossible to forgive her; only good manners and thought for his own professional position made him accept the explanation with a polite bow and a shrug.

In the coach, as they re-assembled there, Rose met nothing but expressions of relief and congratulation. Most of them were astonished. An old school teacher doing a circus act? Where had she learned such a stunt and when? Had she been an Olympic champion in her young days and what at?

She only smiled, told them again, she had been in the W.A.A.F in the war and had always kept fit. Told them again it was lucky she was wearing slacks.

Gwen turned up late as usual. She had been eating an ice in one of the little places off the terrace and had missed seeing the 'Roseanna' party leaving. She did not mention the fact that Owen had plucked her out of the back row of their lot and brought the ice for her and left her eating it while he went off, he said, to have an urgent pee. But he had come back quite soon.

Later that day, talking to Mrs. Banks at the hotel, she heard the story of Rose Lawler's exploit.

"Those friends of hers, Mrs. Donald and Miss Jeans, think she must have been pushed. The crowds were terrible, weren't they?"

Gwen agreed. The crowds had been terrible. It had been terrible too, and exciting, to come across Owen again. She wasn't going to get rid of him in a hurry. But she'd better not confide in Rose yet once more. Because it was more than likely Owen had tried to get rid of her in a hurry.

She sighed. It was difficult to know what to do for the best. Later that evening she put through a call to England from the hotel. This time she took the precaution of sending her message and request for advice in code.

Chapter V

THE 'ROSEANNA' TOUR left Rome the next morning in a
light drizzle that did not begin to lift until noon. This was
a pity because the road passed through particularly beautiful, at times spectacular, country with tall hills covered
with trees to the summit, the limestone rock from which
they sprouted held in at the base where it touched the
road by wide stretches of wire mesh.

But the rain damped down the colours and the contours
and also the spirits of the tourists. Billie tried to rouse
them with some account of the history of this part of
Tuscany, never a peaceful one. But Gwelphs and Ghibel-
lines, their distinctive battlements on their towers, their
never-ending feud, meant nothing at all to the travellers,
who could not be roused until the coach emerged upon
open highway, with Assisi high upon its hill in the distance.

Mrs. Lawler had woken that day very stiff in the legs and
back. She had slept well for several hours from sheer
exhaustion, but had woken before dawn finding it an agony
to turn over, and from then on had suffered with every
move until she had forced herself to get up, take an
aspirin, apply such massage as she could to her own back
and thighs, lie down again and wait with forced patience
for the relief of movement in an upright position.

Sitting in the bus had meant renewed agony for poor
Rose. She could hardly force herself to stand up when

the coach stopped at Assisi in the big car park halfway up the hill. But her friends helped her, though Gwen, after trying to drag her out of her seat without any success, laughed nervously and turning hopped away and down the steps of the coach in front of Mr. Banks, who applied his extra strength to the job of getting Mrs. Lawler upright. Myra and Flo, by easy stages and with much encouragement, did the rest. The tour was to take lunch at an hotel in Assisi and do their sight-seeing in the afternoon. By the time the three women had made a slow march to this hotel Rose declared the walk had done the trick. The stiffness, finally broken, had disappeared.

"It usually goes this way," she declared. "But I didn't realise how bad it was going to be, or I might have done something about it last night before I went to bed."

"What, for instance?" Myra asked.

"Asked you to give me a rub. I take oil about with me even now. But I'd forgotten how much worse it was likely to be at my present advanced age."

The other two exchanged glances.

"I think it is high time, Rose," Flo said, "that you told us what exactly you taught in your schools or what your hobbies were or are that let you perform these Olympic stunts at will."

"Not at will! Sheer necessity! Most unwillingly."

"But what?"

Mrs. Lawler hesitated. She certainly did not want coach gossip, tour gossip, to spread rumours or even true facts about her. To most of them her profession would mean nothing. To be reasonable, to very few indeed of her fellow-travellers. Why did she hesitate? She knew the answer. She had an immediate picture before her eyes of a wrinkled face, a crooked smile, a complete awareness of the meaning of her graceful, successful escape from injury at the Colosseum. But they had left Rome. Oh yes, they had left Rome. And the long black car had not been in the Assisi car park. Or not yet.

"I trained at Bedford," she said quietly. "I was a junior games and gym mistress at one girls' school in the south midlands before the war and at another in the south-west after I was demobbed and my boy started school."

"You were able to pick it all up again?" Myra asked, astonished.

"I did a refresher course. I trained. It was the only thing I could do. I was no good at academic stuff."

"But top-class in your own line," Flo said, admiringly.

There was a short silence. Then Rose said, "Unless anyone wants to know exactly what I taught at schools I'd rather neither of you explained to them."

"They won't," Myra said confidently, "They may have had some sort of P.T., even gym apparatus, but I don't think the hockey or lacrosse games mistress would mean a thing."

"Don't be such a snob," Flo told her.

"Does *that* mean anything these days?" Rose laughed. "Snob, anti-snob! All a mix-up of nonsense, isn't it? People trying to fit themselves into a class they want to belong to, or think they belong to, or want other people to think they belong to, or . . ."

"Stop!" Myra cried. "My head's spinning!"

Gwen Chilton arrived almost first at the hotel. She had been hurrying, partly from fear, but chiefly from curiosity. Owen had told her he would keep in touch but he had not said where he would see her next. It was like him to go to the catacombs, frightening her half out of her wits; coming up behind her, not to pinch her bottom as the Italian boys did, but to whisper in her ear, wanting to know what the old schoolmarm snooper was doing in the garden up above instead of down here where he'd expected.

"She's done this place before. She just wanted to rest in the shade, she said," Gwen had told him.

"Rest, my arse," he breathed, making her giggle.

"Hers, you mean."

"Don't be rude, darling."

Heads turned in their direction. Owen slipped into the darkness, but was soon at her ear again.

"I shall keep in touch," he whispered this time and she felt fingers at her neck as well as breath on her ear. "So don't get tangled with the old bitch or we'll have to eliminate her."

He had gone after this and did not appear again until they were leaving the Colosseum that afternoon. Having made sure she was out of sight of the staircase.

So was Rose Lawler's spectacular descent set off by Owen? Several of the tour had asked her if Mrs. Lawler had been pushed? She could truthfully say she did not know, but it wouldn't be surprising, would it? These crowds do push, don't they?

But she had a shrewd idea it had been Owen, pushing deliberately. Especially since, that very morning, a small man had pressed a note into her hand as she left the Rome hotel. She had slipped it into her bag and now looked forward to reaching the Assisi lunch hotel before the rest of their lot, to open the note in the safe privacy of the toilet.

Owen had written briefly: "Meet me Assisi 2.00 p.m. upper church." He had not signed it or even addressed it in any way inside or out. So how had the little man known her? She shivered, feeling eyes about her in every direction, all her movements watched, enemies ready to pounce at every stage, upon each day of what should have been a safe, if boring, interval in a carefully planned operation.

But she pulled herself together, as she always had done and so far with more than reasonable success. When she joined the three egg heads, as she now thought of them, she was her most controlled shy self, no trace of the false hysteric who had caused them so much embarrassment from time to time.

Rose Lawler could only tell herself that Rome had done Gwen good and that must really be Owen Strong's doing. Time would show if his pursuit of the girl was genuine.

They would know that if he turned up in Florence. In the meantime she and her friends had much to enjoy and would not be hampered by guides other than their Baedekers and maps.

Gwen did not offer to join them. The four had coffee together in the hotel lounge, but when Myra, Flo and Rose took up their handbags and cameras with purposeful glances at one another and a polite question to her, she shook her head, getting out a fresh cigarette to light from the stub she took from her lips. They left her sitting there, staring out of the window, making no sign even to those members of the tour who remarked upon her strange inertia as they passed her.

"I can't make out that young woman at all," Myra said as they climbed the hill slowly towards the church. "Can you, Rose?"

"Not really," Mrs. Lawler answered. Her own thoughts were too fantastic to be shared.

Until, in one of the darker recesses of the first church, she passed a stooping figure that she recognised. For a couple of seconds she thought of accosting him, but then recoiled from the impulse and passed on. This was helped by Flo, who asked her from behind where it was they expected to find certain of the famous Giotto paintings of the life of the Saint. When she had confirmed the answer from her guide book she looked round again, but Owen Strong had disappeared.

He had been startled, waiting in his dark corner, to see Mrs. Lawler at all. Her exploit at the Colosseum, that he had admired as much as he deplored its success and his own consequent failure had, so Rollo had told him, certainly crippled the woman, if only temporarily. So he had judged it safe to have a word with Gwen in Assisi. He had no doubt she had got his note. Rollo never let him down over simple little jobs of communication, especially as the bread-line journalist had been done out of an expected scoop, "Englishwoman falls at Colosseum" by the heroine of the episode from her hospital bed, or an obituary if that was the alternative.

Yet she was here, no more crippled than the rest of that lot with their obvious arthritis, obesity and corns, he thought contemptuously, watching the mixed tourist crowd, waiting for Gwen.

When she came at last, saw him, went to look at a picture near him, waited until his voice at her ear, as in the catacombs said quietly, "Go back to the entrance. I'll join you outside," he moved away at last and Mrs. Lawler, who had seen Gwen arrive, guessed the whole of the subsequent action, though she did not stay to watch it.

The three friends enjoyed the frescoes in the second church, returned to buy postcards in the entrance of the first and then set off into the little town to look at the many shops full of Assisi embroidery worked upon cloths of many sizes and upon clothes for women and children. The patterns were charming, they decided, but the linen upon which they were embroidered was mostly rather poor and the threads uneven in the warp and weft so that the embroidery was not based, as it should be, on squares of counted threads but must have been worked upon a printed outline, quite another thing altogether.

Flo declared she did not mind how they were done they were so pretty and bought a dress for a small niece. But Myra, who had made table mats for herself in the correct manner upon Irish linen, refused to buy, while Mrs. Lawler, whose legs were beginning to ache again, left her friends to walk slowly back to the coach, taking photographs on the way.

When Gwen joined Owen at the door of the church he led her at once up a narrow street that came out behind the top end of the large car park. Here, almost hidden from every direction was the long black car she recognised. He unlocked it and motioned her inside. She recoiled from the oven heat of the interior.

56

"Get in," he insisted. "I want to talk to you."

She was repelled by this rough order.

"You can't take that tone with me!" she cried. "And I'm not going to be roasted to suit your convenience, so you can get that straight."

He realised he had gone too far, too fast. This bird gave an impression of weakness but he really knew already that it was false.

Without speaking he wound down all the windows. The car may have been in the sun when he parked, but it was now in the shade and though the air of the early afternoon had not cooled at all, where the car stood was at the top of the hill and a breeze did blow through it to replace the over-heated air.

"How about that?" he said gently, looking at her with far from gentle eyes.

Gwen accepted the meaning of the look and climbed in, though she shot up from the seat at once, crying out that the leather had burned her. With silent patience Owen pulled forward a cushion from the back seat for her to sit on, then got in himself on the other side. His intention was as firm as ever, but he understood that he had no easy job before him.

Gwen was flattered by his persistence. Her natural vanity had always been a danger to her, and for some months now it had not been fed to anything like the extent she required. Or so she often told herself.

So Owen's cautious approach was unexpectedly successful, he found. Before long he was able to slide an arm behind her shoulders and allowed to leave it there until he dared to move it where the effect could be greater.

"I had to see you again," he murmured, truthfully. "You aren't angry with me?"

"No," she whispered, accepting this familiar approach. "But how did you know we'd be here? Who was that funny little man in Rome?"

"My messenger? Rollo? A journalist who does me a favour now and then."

"Journalist!"

He felt her pull away, so held her more closely.

"Do you mind that? Why should you? Scared of the Press? He's only free-lance and not often employed, I should think."

Allowing his curiosity a too free rein he added, laughing a little in his almost soundless fashion, "I guarantee he never leaves the Imperial City. He is never in Geneva, for instance."

This time she did not pull away; she froze. He cursed himself for his impatience, but he must discover soon what had taken her to that bank, for the expenses were mounting up and if it wasn't going to be worth it he ought to pull out rather than plan ahead to Florence, where he no longer had reliable contacts since . . .

"You asked me that time you walked out on me . . ."

"I never . . ."

"You asked me what was I doing in Geneva myself that time I saw you taking a heavy suitcase into a certain bank and coming out of the bank again to throw the case into a taxi as if it weighed nothing at all."

This time Gwen drew herself right away from him and he had the good sense to let her go. Besides, she had not lost her head and he wanted very much to discover how she would deal with these cards on the table now between them. Quite a girl this, quite a girl!

Gwen, fully back on her dignity, sought some reason for this apparently reckless disclosure. She remembered the tale she had told before. Mistress of her selfish boss for eleven years, fed up with short trips abroad as his wife and no promise of any real status. Ran out on him with any money she could pick up. That was it. The firm's money and quite a lot of it . . . in cash. Mostly one pound notes and you needed a lot of those to make it worth while.

But to think he had spotted her and watched her go in and come out again with the empty case. So what was his game? Pretty obvious, surely? A blackmailer? Or just a con man? Ready to demand the ransom or ready with some scheme to enlarge it for her, for them both, with him working at her side?

A most unwelcome complication, anyway. She picked up her handbag from the floor of the car where it had fallen and felt for the door handle.

"You were there in Geneva and you were watching me, you say," she began. "I can guess why. To latch on to anyone leaving a bank who might be easy meat for your sort. Well, I'm not, see. So you may as well pack it in. I don't want to see you in Florence or anywhere else. And it's time I got back to the coach, see. So goodbye and thank you for nothing."

He sat watching her, not speaking, a little pale. His hands shook on the wheel, so he took them off and held them together in his lap until she had gone. She had made him lose his temper again, but he had been able to confirm one point. She had indeed taken money into that bank, to make a deposit account or add to one already there. Was it her late firm's money or was that tale as phoney as so much of what she said? But the point had been made and accepted. Gwen Chilton had a deposit account at a Swiss bank. It was up to him to make her disgorge it in his favour.

He watched her turn to look about her when she shut the door of the car. He watched her go up into the courtyard before the church and start down again towards the car park where the tourist coaches were standing. Then he turned his car and drove through the car park himself and away down the road to join the autostrada in the plain.

He wore his dark glasses as he drove and a floppy sun hat that covered his thinning hair and creased forehead. He did not look up at all at the narrow road twisting down from the old town where Mrs. Lawler leaned on the

59

parapet to get her breath and to take a distant view of the white church of St. Francis.

But she saw the long black car and took a quick snap of it, almost head on, right in the foreground of her view. The number will be out of focus, she thought, as she put the camera away. Not that it has any importance to me. But to Gwen? What a silly girl, to encourage the man!

Chapter VI

THE TOUR STAYED that night in Perugia. Gwen Chilton
spent a considerable time making her usual telephone call,
but this time to Paris, not London. She felt much happier
when she had finished, so her table companions found her
unusually talkative at dinner. Apart from these three no
one was paying much attention to Mrs. Chilton, except
indirectly, though Rose Lawler was not the only one who
had noticed her leaving the church at Assisi with a man.

"It was the one who directed us at Siena right at the
start, wasn't it?" Mr. Woodruff said, with certainty.

"I couldn't swear to it myself," Mr. Blundell said, with
slight contempt. "I didn't take all that notice."

"Well, I did," his wife announced in her pleasant country
voice. "He was in Rome, too. Quite a romance, by the
look of it."

"Not a very nice one, I wouldn't think," Mrs. Woodruff
added. "Where's her husband? Dead, divorced, or
neither?"

This brought the subject to a stop. Either the man or
the woman would have enjoyed pursuing it further without
the other sex, but neither couple cared to go into more
intimate speculation in company. Besides, another piece
of gossip was engaging the majority of 'Roseanna's' party.

Two carabinieri had been seen at the hotel reception desk
with Mr. Banks. He had left the building with them but

had come back in time for dinner. Mrs. Banks had joined him in the lounge, but not Penny. None of the family appeared for the meal. Rumour, added to previous speculation, was now confirming a suspicion that the girl was indeed smoking cannabis quite freely and frequently and it had got round to the authorities.

The highly respectable majority of 'Roseanna's' tourists were shocked. They discussed the matter in much the same way they were accustomed to talk about juvenile courts at home. An area of public concern and action that was really foreign to them, but also mildly exciting as long as it did not include anyone they knew. When it did, as now, and if anything was to happen to this hippy-like girl, they would state they neither knew nor had seen anything they recognised as criminal.

"Children like to follow the fashion," at least six of the stouter matrons said mildly.

"You'd think the parents did too," said another. "No control these days. I thank my stars mine are all grown-up and settled in good positions."

"Lucky you! We wouldn't have been able to come away if it wasn't for the school cruise to Madeira."

"Mixed?"

"You mean the schools? Well, yes. But then my three are all at the same comprehensive. Ever so good. We're delighted with it, aren't we, Arnold?"

"It's all right. So far. The Head can't possibly know them all — more than a thousand."

"Do they have this drug problem? What we're talking about."

"Are we? How should I know?"

It was noticeable, after dinner, that the coach party split into two main groups; those who really wanted to talk about Assisi, its buildings and pictures, and those who were concerned with Gwen and her new friend or old acquaintance or whatever he was, or else with the Banks' problem. Of these there was the largest, speculative group, throwing out unsupported theory and melodrama and the smaller malicious, strict sectarian, puritan caucus that had been shocked straightaway at Genoa by Penny Banks' appearance and had plotted ever since to get rid of her.

And had now, perhaps, succeeded. They discussed all the disgraceful, sordid symptoms, finding them exhibited by this slatternly girl; they speculated over supplies, pushers, the smuggling trade with the Near and Middle East. By the end of the evening they were resigned to seeing an announcement before long in all the newspapers of the world telling of Penny Banks' arrest.

Before Gwen left her table companions after taking coffee with them in the bar lounge she said, "I was in the hall when the ambulance came for Penny Banks. I don't suppose you were down then. It was just after we got the keys for our rooms."

"No," Rose said. "I wondered a little when she wasn't at dinner. But she often misses meals, doesn't she? An ambulance? Is she really ill, then?"

"Billie said not to spread it. She's going round the others later, she said, in their rooms."

Rose looked at her friends: they all exchanged glances and nodded.

"I've been done for everything," Myra said. "What is it, Gwen? Typhoid?"

Mrs. Chilton, who had been immunised, much against her will, for everything including diphtheria and yellow fever, the year before, stared at them in some horror.

"You're a cool lot, I must say," she said at last.

"No," Rose told her. "We were all advised to be done before we went abroad the first time, years and years ago. Never drink tap water on the continent. Beware of salads et cetera. You still haven't told us what Penny's trouble is."

"Billie asked me if I'd been inoculated. I said yes, was it one of those the Banks girl had got. She said it might

63

be. They'd had an Italian doctor to her and he'd ordered her away."

"Poor girl!" said Flo. "Would that account for the carabinieri with Mr. Banks?"

"That or the pot," Gwen said carelessly. Then, seeing the others' faces she added, "Don't tell me you didn't realise she was hooked? Everyone on the coach seems to know."

"Or think they do," Rose said.

"Well, I'd say I knew," Gwen answered stubbornly. "We've got another of these bloody early starts, haven't we? Florence for lunch, Billie said."

She walked away from them, irritated by their mixture of strange innocence and superior sophistication. This really wasn't the right tour for them. What would be, though? She turned aside on her way to the lifts, obeying a signal from a South London suburban couple she had chatted with in one of the Assisi shops. They had noticed the ambulance, too, and wanted to ask if she knew whether it related to their own party or some other.

Gwen stalled. She felt she did not know them well enough to declare her knowledge. Let them get the shock from Billie. If they did not leave the tour at once she would have another chat with them the next day.

Dragging herself out of bed the next morning Gwen was not surprised to find 'Roseanna's' complement diminished, not only by the Banks family and four other couples, who had been placed in quarantine as contacts, but by three other faint-hearted travellers, who had been immunised but did not trust the foreign advice, still less the foreign hospitals if the advice was proved wrong.

It was a subdued group that proceeded on its way to Florence. There was a short stop on the shores of the beautiful Lake Tragimento. Here Rose and her friends walked out along a short pier to take photographs of pale grey islands emerging from the morning mist. But none of this restored those universal fallen spirits. Nor, as the sun conquered the mist at last and they ordered coffee at little tables on the lake shore in the shade of trees could they drag their thoughts and fears from the late-night bombshell.

Until Billie, who had been making a succession of telephone calls, came hurrying round her flock with a beaming face and fresh, relieving news.

"The tests on Miss Banks and all the others are negative," she repeated over and over again. "She is much better. She will be leaving hospital in a day or two."

"And joining us in Florence?" asked Myra, when Billie reached the table where she and her friends were eating ices.

Billie looked uncomfortable. It was a change from the face of gloom she had worn at breakfast and on the drive to the lake, but the question seemed to have ended her temporary euphoria.

They did not press her, nor did Gwen ask any difficult questions. As for the rest, by the time 'Roseanna' reached Florence the Banks family and the other defectors might never have existed.

The new hotel was one of a series of recent buildings lining a new road along the bank of the Arno river and about a mile out from the centre of the city. Buses just round the corner of the hotel ran frequently, Billie told them. But this afternoon, for those who preferred to leave the tourist crush and heat of the city centre, there was a trip to Fiesole, the little hill town with its church, old houses and ancient Roman theatre, baths and museum.

Gwen was the first to see Owen Strong again. She had joined her table companions at Fiesole for want of something better to do. Their main objective in going there was to see the Roman remains, combined as they were with glorious views of the Apennines, since the excavations lay on the slopes behind the church.

Owen was in the museum peering at a collection of Etruscan pottery in a tall case. He could see the coach party in the glass of the case as they walked into the building, so he did not turn but waited to see what they would do. Particularly Gwen. He hoped his entirely open approach this time would shake her. And fox the three old witches, as he now called them to himself.

He was only partially successful. For one thing he had not reckoned on Gwen's temper, though by now he should have done so. She was furious at seeing him there, in open pursuit of herself. She said loudly to her friends as they all drew near, "Why, isn't that Mr. Strong? Looking at those red and black vases? I'm almost sure of it."

They were just behind him now; he could not pretend he was not aware of them. So he turned slowly, allowing a surprised smile to twist his face into that of an amiable clown. The sight, though by now familiar enough, had its full effect upon Mrs. Lawler. Oh damn, she thought miserably. Memory, never yet more than half submerged, carried her back to the ruined faces of those pilots of the Second War who had survived their martyrdom. Her own love one of the worst, rescued, fought for, but dying at last in final defeat. Even now she could be made to remember that struggle and that end, to feel the guilt and pity and terror of that air war as she had known it.

"Well, fancy seeing you here!" Gwen was saying, glaring at Owen in fully hostile greeting.

"Good afternoon, Mr. Strong," Rose said and turning to her companions went on, "I don't think you've met before. Mrs. Donald, Miss Jeans. Mr. Strong came to our assistance in Siena over finding the duomo."

"And crops up like a bad penny all along the line," said Gwen cheerfully.

There was no easy answer to this, nor did he attempt to find one. Strangled giggles got them nowhere, so he turned to Gwen, as if continuing a conversation only just at that moment interrupted.

"Don't let me forget to give you ..." he began, taking

66

her by the elbow and beginning to guide her towards the door of the museum.

She was too surprised to resist him, but moved where he led until outside in the glare of the sunlight, he dropped her arm to put on his dark glasses. They went down a long flight of steps, moved past a succession of low stone walls, clambered up a steep bank and sank to the brown turf under a clump of wizened bushes.

"You've got a nerve, I must say!" Gwen panted, trying to mop her face with a very small handkerchief, then throwing the wet ball from her in disgust.

"I've been thinking," Owen said. "I'd have tried to contact you earlier, only you had that scare night before last."

"The Banks girl, you mean? So you heard about that? Another of these phoney journalists?"

Owen laughed delightedly.

"No. Actually I have friends in Perugia."

"You always have friends. Never mind. It wasn't typhoid after all."

"It never was typhoid. But it wasn't heroin, after all, either. Just a silly kid, smoking pot. Overdid it. Your driver made a statement."

"I'm not surprised. She socked him one the time she hurt her foot trying to kick Mrs. Lawler and getting the coach steps instead because the old girl was too quick for her."

He frowned, hearing that name. But he only said, "So that was why your Mario turned her in? Ities don't like being attacked by women." He moved closer to her and said, "Forget all that dreary lot. Let me drive you back into Florence."

Cooled and rested Gwen let him stroke her arm. His hand was cold and dry; when presently he began to kiss the arm and then her neck and finally her mouth, his lips too were dry and cool, less than eager, but surprisingly compelling. She felt too lazy and far too comfortable to

67

resist these advances; which surely could go no further in this place where people moved to and fro below and above the shrubs where they were sitting. But she still wondered at his appearance in Fiesole, so openly, even advertising his arrival.

"Obvious," he answered her question. "Rome was a washout. Mrs. Lawler suspects me of having designs on you. I bet you've encouraged her."

"I had to."

"Granted So the best thing is for me to play the open-handed, open-hearted bum, out bird-catching. At your age the old hags will decide you can, must, or ought to look after yourself, so — "

"Thanks very much," Gwen said, roused from apathy by this picture of the proceedings. "I suppose the next move is to find Billie and tell her I'm off now, but will be back at the hotel for dinner."

"Exactly."

He got up in one easy movement, lifted her to her feet in another and brushed her down first before giving her a final and much warmer kiss.

"You go ahead and I'll have the car outside the church in five minutes, flat."

Billie took Gwen's nonchalant message in the matter-of-fact spirit in which it was given. If Mrs. Chilton and her ageing admirer were making progress in this girl and boy fashion, it was not for her to laugh at the poor old things, only make sure they did not shock the respectable clientele, already a bit shaken by the false typhoid scare. She decided she would not spread the news of Gwen's action. Time enough, when the coach party assembled and voices began to report Mrs. Chilton's disappearance, to announce that she had gone ahead with friends.

"Mr. Strong, obviously," Mrs. Lawler said. "Well, if she chooses to behave like a silly child, who are we to try to stop her?"

Myra and Flo agreed.

Owen drove to a garage on the outskirts of Florence, where he parked his car and suggested they might walk to his hotel.

"Is it near?" Gwen asked, looking up at the sky. The change there had been dramatic. She had seen the black patch on the horizon from the steps of the church where Owen was waiting. No more than a patch it had been, and he had laughed when she pointed it out and told her it might hit the coach but they would be ahead of it all the way down and it would probably miss Florence altogether.

"Is what near?" Owen asked a little irritably.

"This hotel of yours?"

"Reasonably. I thought you meant the storm."

He was looking up himself now and then down to where a few black wet patches, the size of saucers, had appeared on the wide pavement.

"Ow!" Gwen cried as a similar giant drop fell on her upturned face and spread out on every side.

"Run!" Owen said, taking her arm and starting off himself.

There was no time for protest, no point in argument. The sky had opened, the lightning flashed, the thunder rolled, the people ran and jumped and scurried, scarves and jackets and newspapers clamped over their heads. They dashed across streets where the wash from cars and vans splashed them to their knees; they stepped down from pavements into ankle deep ponds; they waded through shallow fast-flowing streams. Gwen had no idea where they were going but Owen continued to hold her arm and urge her on with cries of "Run, darling! Keep it up! Run!"

When at last he stopped in the shelter of the dark little porch of a tall building in a tree-lined street, she panted, "I can't go on! I'm soaking! I can't breathe! I must rest!"

He released her arm to pat her shoulder.

"So you shall, love. We've arrived. We're here. Shall we go inside?"

She looked about her. There were glass doors at the back of the porch and lights behind them. Water was running from her hair down her face and down the back of her neck. Her thin sleeveless dress was clinging to her, drips from it running down her bare muddy legs to her filthy, squelching sandals.

"I can't!" she protested. "I'm a sight! I'm not fit to be seen!"

She found she was shivering and began to cry.

"Come on," Owen said roughly. "I'm as bad as you. We've got to dry off and warm up. They'll fix us inside."

"I want a taxi," Gwen insisted. "I want to go back to my own hotel."

"Taxi! You've got a hope! Don't be daft! Come inside."

She knew he was right. She might have known when she left Fiesole that it would all fall out like this. She had let him take control then and the thunderstorm had merely helped him. In any case it would explain her delay in reaching the hotel on the Arno.

Owen proved to be a grand fixer. His room was reasonably good like the one in Rome. Her clothes disappeared to be cleaned and dried and she didn't need them. The shower was warm and Owen, afterwards, completely restored her circulation. Her response encouraged him.

He began to talk about the strange chance that had brought them together.

"Chance?" Gwen laughed indulgently, stroking his bare shoulder. "You know you followed me."

"I didn't know you'd turn up at Genoa. I swear I didn't."

He waited, but she did not answer so he said softly, "Why did you come on this tour, my darling? Why not stay in Switzerland? Why not move the lolly right away, once it was safely stowed? Why not play it cool and fast?"

She drew away from him.

"Why are you asking all this?"

He pulled her back and began to kiss her again, talking between caresses.

"Because I think you need help. You're in a mess. You've nicked your firm's petty cash, or so you told me in Rome, to revenge yourself on your boss who won't marry you. And you don't know how to go on from that. But you know you can't go back to England. Are they watching for you there? Has he put the Law on you? He must know the safe's empty. He must have taken *some* action."

"No!" Gwen cried, sitting up and covering her ears to shut out all these questions. "You've got it all wrong! From start to finish! I was only the messenger!"

"*What!*"

Owen was up now, staring down at her.

"You were...! Then boss — lover-boy — or not the real boss... That's the one that filled the heavy suitcase and had you carry the can to Geneva? Was that it?"

Gwen nodded miserably. Anything to stop him asking questions she could never really answer. Anything... anything...

Chapter VII

GWEN HAD, AS usual, a plausible story for her long delay in getting back to the hotel on the Arno. Owen's car had been slowed down by the traffic when the storm broke. They had crawled into the town at last, but at a big junction of roads, where water from blocked drains had formed a lake, their engine had been drowned as Owen tried to slip past near the kerb. They had to run for his hotel, getting soaked in the process. But the management had been most helpful. While she was put into a room to wait for her dress and things to be dried quickly, Owen had gone off to rescue his car with the help of his garage.

"He was lucky," Rose said. "We saw a lot of breakdowns on our own way back."

Gwen smiled.

"He speaks the language and seems to have plenty of money."

"That would help certainly. So he was able to bring you back here?"

"Oh no!" Gwen opened wide, innocent eyes. "The car was towed to the garage to be dried out. I came home in a taxi."

"Another piece of luck," said Flo. "But of course you speak the language, too."

"And with Mr. Strong to help . . ." Rose left it at that while the meal lasted. But afterwards, sipping their usual coffee, she said in a low voice to Gwen, "My dear, are you feeling better about this Mr. Strong? I mean, you were so worried in Rome. And he does seem to be following you. In Assisi..."

"How d'you know he was in Assisi?"

The girl's voice was sharp, quite unnecessarily so, Rose thought, but she answered the question calmly.

"Because I saw his car leaving. Actually, it came into my viewfinder when I was taking a last photograph on my way down to the car park."

"You took a photo of his car... with him in it?"

Gwen was excited, but suppressed any show beyond mild interest.

"Yes. I've been taking pictures all along the line, you know. For the first few days not deliberately of our lot. But I'm sure you'll figure in several of them. You shall have a look later on when they're developed. They're colour slides, so the prints are not terribly good. But you're very photogenic, my dear, as you must know by now."

She regretted adding "by now" for Gwen might take offence, even at such a mild reference to her age.

Mrs. Lawler sighed, thinking about the silly rules concerning age that seemed to govern all the conversation on the tour. Age and sex. A dreary convention of un-funny jokes and sniggers.

She pulled herself up. Her own censorious attitude was equally tiresome. Who was she to prefer the sort of indecent wit that made her laugh. Who indeed!

Gwen, regarding her friend now with terrified awe, entirely missed the reference to her age. But she soon calmed herself, for she found she could not remember any single occasion when Mrs. Lawler's camera could possibly have compromised her. Her memory did not go back to the little square in San Gimignano and the bank where she had used her Swiss passport.

On further consideration she began to see some profit

73

in Rose's collection of pictures, providing she could secure the sole use of them for herself. Or at least of those of Owen and his car. How to do this was difficult but she decided to think about it.

Her thoughts were given an added incentive the next morning. She had gone out early to buy a newspaper, an Italian one, because English papers always appeared at least a day later than their printing and so two days later than the events set down in them.

On the second page of her Italian news sheet there was a blurred picture, small, but familiar. Owen's car. Or rather, not Owen's car, but that of an irate owner, whose car had been taken from a park in Nice, just ten days ago. The number was different, the make was a common one, English with a right-hand drive. But somehow Gwen felt it was Owen's car, in a snapshot taken with its real owner, wearing its real number plate, not the substitute he had put on it.

So what about those photographs that Rose Lawler had taken? If she could lay her hands on them she had a definite good new hold over Owen. She could stop him badgering her, trying to con her into sharing that valuable asset so safely stashed away in the Swiss bank.

She frightened herself with several nasty guesses of what he might do to her when she disclosed her new power. But she would play it as cool as she knew how. She need not tell him what her evidence was that would bring the police of several nations upon him. She would just make it clear that she could do that if she had to. But in the meantime they could go on with an association that was so very pleasant that it could well begin to weaken her resolution if she continued it too ardently.

Gwen checked her thoughts. That wouldn't do, to fall for Owen in a big way. Look how it had turned out with Jake.

That sobered her, the thought of Jake. She looked up at Mrs. Lawler, knowing she had been silent for far too long.

"Oh well," she said. "He is rather attractive and I don't think there's really any harm in him. Not real harm. Do you?"

Mrs. Lawler found this speech so palpably false and the implied "harm" so vulgar, so twisted, that she could not help laughing in an unmirthful way that Gwen did not understand, but took to be reassuring.

The programme of sight-seeing for the next day was a formidable one. As Rose said to her friends at breakfast, "We're in for the whole Renaissance today. Together with the other thousands of tourists. I'm terrified, frankly."

"What of?" Myra was curious; this was not like Rose.

"Of being disappointed — disillusioned. Of being forced to say to myself, 'Yes, I know this picture. I've been seeing reproductions of it for fifty years and the original barely come up to them, or doesn't even come up to them . . .'"

"Blasphemy!" exclaimed Flo. "I should be angry if I thought you meant it, but of course you don't. What time do we start?"

Rose told her and left the table to avoid more argument. She had only half meant what she said, but there was a small element of truth in it. Her inner confusion lasted until it was time to join the coach, which meant that she had to hurry down the stairs instead of waiting for the rather slow service of the lift. 'Roseanna's' complement had arrived in the hall in a block, talking and laughing and dropping their keys on the reception desk as they passed it.

Mrs. Lawler joined them to put down her own key, turning as she did so to find Gwen at her shoulder.

"So you're coming, after all?" she said.

"Of course," Gwen answered. "Look there! Billie's waving at us to buck up."

Billie was doing no such thing, Rose decided, but she did not contradict, only went forward quickly. Gwen dropped her room key on the desk, picked up Mrs. Lawler's and stuffed it into her handbag. She climbed into the coach directly behind her friend and sat down, breathing rather quickly.

"Well, at least there doesn't seem to be another thunderstorm on the way," she said as they started.

"Thank heaven for that," Rose answered. "Are you expecting Mr. Strong to turn up again as it's fine?"

Gwen was not disturbed.

"Not really. The engine of his car stalled in a deep puddle yesterday. I told you that, didn't I? It would have to be dried out, wouldn't it?"

"Perhaps. I don't know much about cars."

"And you in the W.A.A.F.! Driving, weren't you?"

"Well, no. I was in a radar section. Taking down results. Nowadays the computer would do it all, I suppose."

The subject flagged, the coach made its skilful way to the duomo, where they all got out. Sight-seeing began in earnest.

In spite of her misgivings that morning and later at the Uffizi gallery, Rose was neither disappointed nor disillusioned. The great works of art, in architecture, painting and sculpture moved and excited her as she had not believed they could do any longer. Afterwards she had to admit that she had not noticed when Gwen Chilton had left her side. But neither could Myra or Flo name a time.

"She was with us when we were crowding in to get a look at the Baptistry doors. I remember seeing her there," Myra said firmly.

"That was quite early on. At the Pitti Palace, then?"

"No. I don't believe she was with us, then."

"What about you, Flo?"

"I think I did see her at the Pitti. Does it matter?"

They were walking in a group, behind others of their tour, on their way now to a leather shop where they were to be shown the craft of decorating various leather articles with intricate patterns in gold leaf. An ancient craft, they were told, with traditional designs. Clearly an invitation to buy souvenirs and gifts.

"I think I've had enough for one morning," Rose said, suddenly. "But you two carry on. I'm going back for an hour's rest before lunch. I want to be able to join the trip out to Monte Scenario this afternoon."

She did not wait for replies or reproaches or argument, but seeing what appeared to be an empty taxi at the kerb, she ran quickly to it, got inside and gave her instructions. The driver, accustomed to tourists, set off at once.

Rose's impulse was not without foundation. She had not seen Gwen's actual departure from their group but she thought it could not have been many minutes before she missed her. It must have been when they were all walking, led by their guide, from the region of the Pitti Palace to that of the leather shop.

So there were two questions to which she must find an answer. Had Gwen left to join Owen again, keeping an appointment made with him the afternoon before? Or had she suddenly caught sight of him and run away to meet him or to avoid him? And if the latter, since it was the obvious place of refuge, gone back to the hotel?

Arrived there, standing at the reception desk asking for her key, a third solution presented itself. For her key was not on the rack.

"I left it on the desk here," Rose insisted.

"The senora must be mistaken. It is not in her bag?"

"It is not."

"The senora saw it placed on the hook?" He turned round to put his finger in the appropriate empty place.

"No. We were all a little late for getting into the coach. We put our keys down for you people to cope with after we'd left."

Most of this speech she spoke in English, far too fast and idiomatic for the desk attendant. He shrugged and said nothing.

"Perhaps my friend, Mrs. Chilton, is in her room?" Rose said, her third surmise about Gwen growing in conviction. She gave the number, for she had learned it the

77

day before, since her room was on the same floor and only a few doors from Gwen's own.

"The signora's key is not here, either," the man said.

His assistant, who had followed the foregoing exchange with some interest, came nearer to explain that the Signora Chilton had taken her key only a few minutes before.

"Thank you," Mrs. Lawler said. "Please go on looking for my key. I suppose there will be a room maid upstairs on my floor?"

"Si, si, signora," the two men assured her, glad to be rid of her, convinced she would find her key, retrieved by the staff, in the door of her room.

There was no reply to her knock on Gwen's door. But she did not really expect it. She found one of the floor maids, explained what she wanted in her halting but careful Italian and walked with her back to her own door. The maid turned the lock, pushed open the door and stood aside for Rose to pass her.

Gwen Chilton was on her knees beside Rose's larger suitcase. She had the lid thrown back and was rummaging in the pockets of the case.

"Well, Gwen," Mrs. Lawler said in an icy voice. "I must say I didn't expect *this*!"

Which was a lie because she had half expected something of the sort ever since she had remembered in the taxi that she had told Gwen the night before about the photographs she had taken of Owen Strong, or rather of his long black car.

The maid, terrified by the menace in the English lady's voice and the chalk-white stricken look upon the other's, summoned enough courage to ask faintly, "The key, signora?"

"Is here in the lock, thank you," said Mrs. Lawler, and giving her a gentle push into the corridor, shut the door on her, locked it from the inside and put on the catch that would defeat any further attempted entry.

Having put the key into her handbag Rose turned and

said, "You'd better get up, Gwen, and sit down and tell me what you think you're doing. Incidentally, how did you manage to undo my case? I left it locked."

As Gwen continued to kneel, trembling all over, her mouth fallen open, Rose stepped up to her and bending down pulled a small bunch of keys from one of the locks of the suitcase. After giving it a surprised look, she dropped it into her handbag beside the hotel room key.

The action brought Gwen scrambling to her feet, her colour returning at what she felt was an outrage.

"That's mine!" she cried.

"Hardly," Rose answered. She wondered if the little thief had a weapon, wondered too if her superior physical skills could find any place against a sudden outburst of rage and fear from a desperate young woman.

She moved quickly to the bedside and laid her hand on the telephone.

"Go over to that chair by the window and sit down," she ordered, "or I shall call the police."

She had no idea, really, how this could be done, but it was a phrase that every Englishman knew from childhood. She hoped it would work.

Gwen was not alarmed by the phrase since she knew it would *not* work, or not as Mrs. Lawler intended. Indeed, probably in a contrary manner. But she must get her own keys back and she must pacify the old girl, which meant explaining why she had done this very unfortunate thing. How the devil had the old bitch guessed? She must have second sight? Or had she seen...? And then pretended...?

"Well, go on! Explain!" Mrs. Lawler urged. "Or would you rather...?"

She picked up the receiver, but put it down when Gwen held out an imploring hand.

"No. No please Mrs. Lawler — Rose! I — I must have asked for the wrong room number!"

"Rubbish! The desk would have corrected you!"

"I — I meant to keep my key with me, so I put it in my bag. Only it was yours I picked up . . ."

"Yes. You picked up my key as we left and kept it in your bag. But you didn't think it was yours, for you asked for yours when you came in. They told me so at the desk."

Gwen began to cry, not noisily, but as she always did, tears running pathetically down pale cheeks, at first individual large round tears, later a delicate stream caught in, then overflowing, a small limp handkerchief.

"Stop that!" Mrs. Lawler said, contemptuously. "You stole my key, you left your group on purpose to come here and get into my room. Why? What for?"

"Don't you know?" Gwen said, suddenly seeing a possible way out of this horrible situation. "Don't you remember telling me about the photographs you had taken in Assisi of Owen in that black car. Well, it was in the paper I got this morning. It wasn't his."

"What wasn't his?"

"The car. It gave the owner's name. English tourist on the French Riviera. He stole it. He must have."

"Owen stole that black car? So what?"

She had no wish now to ring up the police. They could get on with their job by themselves. Her threat to Gwen was meaningless but the threat to herself and the man with the war-scarred face was very real. If it depended, as seemed possible, upon photographs she had taken, she must hide them from Gwen. Whatever the girl's real motives in all this, she was a declared thief with her bunch of suitcase keys; not to be trusted ever again.

The immediate need was to get the girl out of her room.

"You don't expect me to believe a word you say now, do you, Gwen?" she said coldly. "You must leave my room at once. If you have taken anything of mine you must put it back first. Before I go through everything."

She looked at her watch.

"I came away from the tour early because I didn't like

80

the way you sneaked off without telling us. You can make what explanation you like at lunch. I shall not contradict you. Now, anything to hand back?"

"No, Rose. I swear I didn't take a thing. I just wanted..."

"My used film. Very well. You may like to know I have already sent my first lot of pictures home to be processed."

"Then the ones of Assisi...? You haven't finished that film yet?"

"Really, Gwen, you don't expect me to tell you that?"

"My keys..."

"If I find there is nothing missing in my case, I will give them back to you at lunch. Now go away before I change my mind and send for Billie and denounce you."

Just like a third-rate historical novel, she thought, Victorian housewife and cringing between-maid.

Gwen, sulky, with downcast eyes, obeyed the command.

Nothing was missing, much to Mrs. Lawler's relief. She tidied the contents of the suitcase, locked it up again and turned to her camera that was lying on the bed where she had thrown it when she discovered Gwen in the room. Fortunately, with the snaps she had taken that morning, there was only one unused picture on the film in it. She wound on to the end, took out the roll of film and put in a fresh one. The used one, safe in its little can, she packed, addressed, stamped and carried down at once to post in the hotel box. How fortunate she had provided herself with the correct postage. How lucky she had followed this plan for her photographs, to avoid having them ruined by an airport inspection for metal in passengers' luggage. If needed, her evidence would be ready for her by the time she got back to England. And she would refrain from taking pictures of cars belonging to doubtful characters. She did not expect to see Owen in the long black car again. What colour would his next one be?

Chapter VIII

IT WAS YELLOW. A very ugly shade of mustard yellow, that might be conspicuously helpful at night to other drivers on the road, but which clashed with almost any landscape.

The car was moving slowly up the hill road when 'Roseanna', climbing magnificently in spite of its great load of tourists, passed it, took a very sharp corner and then turned into a narrow lane, which it blocked completely.

Rose glanced at Gwen by her side but said nothing. The girl had been staring ahead since the coach started; she had made no sign whatever when they passed the yellow car. It was Mrs. Lawler who had looked down and seen and caught a very brief glimpse of the pulled-down panama hat she had recognised at Assisi.

So Owen Strong was again pursuing, not even waiting until his black car was mended. If it was his; if Gwen's almost incoherent story was another of her lying fantasies, as Rose was now inclined to believe. And surely it must be, if Owen could get hold of another car and drive it quite openly. Police methods in these Latin countries might be peculiar; certainly in Italy they seemed to the northern foreigner to be haphazard. But they must be aware of the newspaper story, if it was true there had been one. Gwen could have lied about that, too.

Mrs. Lawler controlled these thoughts when they had completed their unprofitable circuit in her mind for the third time. She transferred her attention to wholly outward things, finding plenty there to occupy her, for the scenery as they climbed the narrow road to the monastery at the summit of the hill was of extraordinary beauty. Mile upon mile, she gazed, as at Fiesole, into a distance of tree-covered mountains, some tall, some no more than hills, with wide fields at their base washed emerald by the recent storm and fading away in the distance to a blue mist where the sun still drew up the rain the thirsty ground had not had time to suck down.

The coach passed through gates guarded by two monks in long black gowns. One or two private cars were drawn up outside the gates, evidently not allowed any further. The occupants, apparently all tourists, perhaps Italian, for they were certainly not peasants, stood in little groups near each of the guards, who carried large sticks with which to control the movements of straying children.

The coach party, deposited in the shade of trees beside the drive, assembled at the foot of a wide flight of steps that led up from the gravel to the entrance doors of the monastery. Billie explained that they would be taken round the establishment by a priest, not a monk, and as he was not sure of his English he would explain to her in Italian and she would translate this.

So they waited, chatting quietly among themselves. They had a new and interesting topic to enliven them, for Mr. and Mrs. Banks and the quarantined couples had joined them again from Perugia. But Penny Banks was still absent. Gwen stood with Mrs. Lawler and her friends. She seemed as apathetic as usual, not sulky, only withdrawn.

Until her sudden, indrawn breath and startled eyes, staring back down the drive, brought the other three to look in the same direction.

Owen Strong was walking towards them, not hurrying, not dawdling, just approaching steadily to an expected appointment, a faint smile lifting the corner of his scarred mouth, dark glasses hiding the eyes that did not share the smile.

"Good afternoon," he said politely as he reached the coach party.

It was addressed to Gwen and her immediate companions, but in a voice loud enough to bring response from the others who had seen him before; notably the Blundells and the Woodruffs.

Gwen said nothing, only drew nearer to Flo Jeans. Mrs. Lawler said, "Good afternoon, Mr. Strong. I thought it was you in the yellow car."

"You passed me," he aswered, not in the least put out. "It doesn't climb like my old 'Success'." He paused, then said, the smile growing to clown width, "I suppose Gwen told you we were half-drowned in the thunderstorm the day before yesterday?"

"Yes. And the car put out of action."

"Only temporarily. They have lent me this yellow job while the drying-out goes on."

At this point Billie reappeared at the top of the steps with a young man in a black sweater and neat black slacks. To the astonishment of the tourists, who had expected an elderly gentleman in gown and biretta, she introduced him as the priest who would act as guide.

By this time the Italians whose cars were parked outside the gates arrived to join the party, so bi-lingual explanations suited them all. Mrs. Lawler said to Owen, "This will be good for my Italian, which is not much more than basic. You speak it fluently I believe."

"Pretty well," he answered quietly.

They all moved up the outside staircase and into the building. Gwen, with a brief greeting, moved away from Owen to join Mr. and Mrs. Banks. She had avoided Myra and Flo since lunch, for that meal had been so awkward, so silent, so embarrassing that she felt sure Rose Lawler had told the others the story of her own exposure in the schoolmarm's room, in spite of her promise not to do so. Mean old cow, seeing she had not taken anything belonging to the old bitch! So she attached herself to the recently returned Banks couple instead, hoping she might perhaps change to their table now that it seemed plain the little camp daughter had left the tour.

"Has Penny gone home after all?" she asked, as the whole party moved into the building.

"Oh no," Mr. Banks answered after a little pause, while Mrs. Banks looked away, apparently concentrating on Billie's translation of the young priest's remarks.

This was not encouraging. Had the girl been taken into custody or just warned off? Had she been charged with having, using or even peddling the cannabis Gwen's nose had already detected, in spite of the opened window in the coach. Had Penny exchanged a hospital bed for a prison cell? If so surely her parents would exhibit rather more emotion over their neglected child? But perhaps not; they were stupid enough to feel very little about anything. Gwen, still smarting from her untimely exposure, was determined to climb back upon the shortcomings of the Banks family to her former hard-won peak of self-confidence.

Owen watched her carefully without at all being suspected of doing so. Why this change in her? What could have happened, apart of course from the fact that she had probably also seen the newspaper paragraph about the car. So had the garage where it was being serviced. But he had no fears over that. He had hired the thing in Nice from friends who ran a very convenient hire service, using vehicles supplied without questions asked by other friends and acquaintances, including himself. If the present garage chose to check the engine number of the black job, he had his hire-car receipt and they in Nice had theirs for buying it, in a wholly fictitious name. And there the search would end unless the irate owner ...

"But you expect the 'Success' to be dried out by tomorrow?" Mrs. Lawler was asking him.

"Oh yes. I don't see why not. I hope so."

"We go to Venice tomorrow," Rose said. "Where do you go next?"

"Venice, of course," he answered, laughing, which made the nearby tourists look round and frown, so she stopped asking questions, only wondered at his persistence in following such an unprofitable quest, a dangerous one perhaps, certainly worthless. Ought she to warn him? No, that would be going too far. And it was not the kind of thing anyone of her generation would consider possible. But Gwen of all people! A little hotel thief ... practised too, with that bunch of suitcase keys! Though she had not time to steal anything from her, herself. With her story of a stolen car, of wanting photographic evidence against Owen! *He* had not behaved like a car thief when he spoke about the "Success" and its present substitute. Far from it.

During the course of the tour inside the building Rose found herself no longer beside Owen, so she joined her friends and stayed with them until they all went out on to a wide terrace.

Here they found again the marvellous views of the Apennines they had enjoyed on the way up the hill. But now spread out on three sides in all their grandeur, row upon row dissolving to the north and east into the blue horizon, falling to the sun-filled south below where the monks cultivated a few acres for the monastery. Beyond lay Florence baking beside the Arno.

Rose swung her camera into position to begin taking pictures. Owen's voice behind her said "May I?" and before she could speak had slipped the strap over her head and taken the camera from her to begin fiddling with the various adjustments.

She was shocked, outraged and suddenly in face of his cool insolence and sleight of hand, afraid. Photographs! Again their possible importance flashed through her mind.

86

She laid her hand upon his which was holding her property as if it were his own, and said as steadily as she could manage: "I have it properly set. This is a new film, so don't mess it up, will you?"

"No," he said. "Of course not. I see it's new. I just want — may I *please* — to take a picture of you and your friends. I left my camera behind this morning. Stupid of me."

He was half laughing, but had moved away from her, still holding her camera, brushing off her hand as if it was no more than a fly, she told herself. And now Myra and Flo were beside her and Gwen just behind them.

"Perfect background," Owen said loudly. "Gwen, come a bit forward. On the parapet side. That's O.K. Now all of you — watch the birdie — say *cheese* — Fine!"

He clicked and wound on and gave the camera back to Mrs. Lawler with a little bow. "I shall expect a print of that," he concluded.

Rose said nothing. Her astonishment, her anger, had freed all those emotions she usually kept locked away where they did not trouble her. But now they were tumbling out to find excuses for him, to forgive his boyish effrontery in a rush of pity for this maimed, middle-aged, lonely man, driving about the Continent looking for — what? Solace, affection, lost gaiety, destroyed happiness, battered health ...

She leaned on the parapet, staring out at the mountains. Gwen and the other two had moved away. But Owen remained.

"I think you must have been in the R.A.F. in the war," she said, speaking with an effort.

He was surprised, but saw that she was very serious and responded to it.

"Yes, I was," he answered.

"In a fighter squadron?"

"Yes."

Feverishly he tried to remember the name of the airfield where he had served, but failed. But it did not matter as she went on speaking.

"You must have been brought down — in flames. Was it over the Channel? Did you manage to get out in time?"

"Yes." He had to play it carefully: he still did not understand what she was driving at. But there could be no harm in asking, "How do you know all that?"

"I don't really. Except that I was in the W.A.A.F and I married a fighter pilot and it happened to him."

"I see." He did not see, so he added, "And so?"

She gathered herself to explain.

"He was burned — very badly — hands and face. And you . . ."

"Ah." The scars, yes, that was what she meant. He might have known. Anyone so observant, such curiosity. Of course that accounted for the morbid interest, damn her.

He forced himself to say gently, "It was a long, long time ago, Mrs. Lawler. The world has forgotten us. I know you can't do that, but I try . . ."

She was crying quietly now, he saw, so he left her, detaching Gwen from the others too and saying to them, "Mrs. Lawler seems to be upset. I hope it wasn't my fault, hijacking her camera."

"Rose!" Myra called, hurrying across the terrace. "Rose, there are two of the sweetest little lizards running round the fountain. Come and look!"

Rose blew her nose, wiped her eyes, fixed her dark glasses more firmly and obeyed. The lizards, about four inches long and very active, were darting about the basin of a small dry fountain at the centre of the terrace, pursued by several tourists who were trying to photograph them in their short periods of rest. It was an unproductive task for the lizards were practically invisible against the stone colour of the fountain and would be hard to see on the sunny side of it and impossible to pick out in the shadow.

Gwen drove back to Florence with Owen, a silent drive for each had a good deal to think about that did not concern the other. Owen put her down at the tour hotel, simply told her to look out for him in Venice and drove away at once. She had meant to warn him about Mrs. Lawler, but he gave her no opportunity, so he must take his chance that the old snooper did no harm, with her prying and watching and obvious suspicions.

That evening after dinner Rose invited Myra to a walk along the Arno. They went to the first of the bridges and leaned on it looking down at the water, which seemed low and far away and sluggish.

"Hardly possible to imagine it up to where we are and more in those floods," Myra said.

"I know. Were you ever here before? I mean can you see any difference?"

"No. And you?"

"It's my first visit too."

Myra looked at her friend. Mrs. Lawler was staring into the distance now, thinking of all those hard years when she had found neither time nor money to think of going abroad and later when she was alone, still working, saving up to join Tim in Canada. A project that died when he announced his marriage and wrote to say he would bring his Mary to visit her in England instead. So far this had not happened either. So she had come to Italy alone and now . . .

All at once she felt she must explain to someone, must justify herself in her present dilemma, must stop the dangerous impulses that were beginning to drive her.

"Myra," she said. "I asked you to come out because if I don't talk to someone I think I shall go round the bend, or get the next plane home or something equally idiotic or desperate."

It was not the first time Mrs. Donald had been appealed to. Problems were common among her Civil Service friends. Wasn't she going about just now with poor Flo, who had been turned down by a late attachment, the bastard. So she said quietly in an encouraging voice, "Go ahead, Rose. Is it about that odd couple, Gwen Chilton and her pick-up?"

"It certainly is."

With thankful relaxation Mrs. Lawler explained her problem. She still did not betray Gwen; she had promised the girl; she would not break the promise. But Owen . . .

"I don't know whether to trust him or not," she said, with desperation in her voice. "Common sense suggests he is some sort of petty crook, though I can't see what he hopes to get out of Gwen. Or me, for that matter. *Did* he push me in Rome? *Did* he try to get hold of my photographs? If I hadn't changed the film would he have taken it? Or spoiled it? There was one snap left. I sacrificed it and took that film out on purpose and sent it to England to be processed. Why did he insist on taking a photo of us three, no four, with Gwen? Will he try to get hold of that one? Why should he? He has a camera of his own. I've seen him with it. Why didn't he bring it to the monastery?"

Her spate of questions had exhausted her. She stopped speaking. Myra saw that she was trembling.

"What I want to know, Rose," she said gently, "is why you're so het up about this Owen Strong, this total stranger."

"Because he makes me think of Charles," Rose answered. "I — I thought I would never . . . But he . . . his poor face . . ."

Her voice trembled now. Myra put a hand on her friend's arm and said, "You have told us how you lost your fighter pilot husband. He was brought down, I suppose?"

"Yes."

90

"And badly burned? Face and hands?"

"Yes. Terribly, terribly, burned."

"And died?" Myra whispered.

Rose jerked back from the bridge parapet.

"No!" she cried in a voice of agony. "No, he *lived*! They saved him and mended him. They were so pleased with themselves. They gave him back to me — an appalling, terrifying grotesque!"

Myra recoiled too, outraged by the welling up of that old horror, that sickened, sickening disgust. But she had lived through those times herself, though as a child. She had heard of this thing and not all the victims' loved-ones had been so appalled.

"You had to keep your feeling for him? You had to pretend? But that can't have been difficult if you loved him."

"If I had truly loved him. I was twenty. I was in love with him — madly, romantically — his looks, his heroism, his lovemaking. If we had both been able to go beyond all this to find our true selves... But we couldn't — we didn't — the hideous mask he now had for a face, and he hated it, it disgusted him, far more than it did me, in the end. I tried, Myra, I truly tried. I did love him. But with Tim on the way by then... No future for Charles in flying, the thing he really loved most... He decided he had no future, so he gave up."

"You don't mean...?"

"Yes. He had tranquillisers, of course. I knew what he was going to do. I didn't take them away. I didn't warn his doctor. I pretended to myself he was going to do the right thing for us all. I did nothing — nothing — to save him."

"When was this? How long after, well, after he left hospital?"

"Five months. He said once he'd never be able to bear the child looking at him."

Mrs. Lawler beat her hand on the stone of the bridge.

"It was my fault! My fault! I try to find excuses. I try to beat down the guilt. And then someone turns up like Owen Strong, grinning like a clown with that stretched false skin on his cheeks and round his mouth and it all comes up again and all I want is to help Owen for Charles's sake, which is ridiculous, isn't it?"

She had talked herself into some sort of control, forcing her thoughts back to the stranger who had, perhaps, relieved her of some part of the pressure that plagued her wherever she went.

Myra waited, knowing there was nothing she could say to heal such a wound, save allow the bitter discharge of this grief to engulf her own mind as it passed from her friend.

At last she said quietly, "Shall we go back to the hotel? We've got an early start for Venice tomorrow, don't forget."

"I had forgotten," Rose answered simply.

They moved away together and hardly spoke on the way back. They said goodnight to one another when they parted outside the lift on the landing of the second floor where each had her room.

"Sleep well," Myra said comfortably as she leaned forward to kiss her friend goodnight.

"I think I shall," Rose answered, acknowledging a debt and giving an assurance that neither, being Englishwomen of a similar restricted upbringing would ever refer to it again.

Chapter IX

THE DRIVE TO Venice was long and tiring, most of the tourists agreed, though as 'Roseanna' went down from the eastern side of the Apennines into the flat lands of the Po delta the continuing rain was left behind, so that by noon the sun shone overhead, the coach warmed up, grew overheated. The roads were dry, the fields with their vines and corn crops shimmered in the sun haze.

At the lunch stop a rather subdued party talked in low voices. Florence had not been a success. The rain and storms, the milling crowds in every place of interest, the infrequent buses and taxis, the language difficulty, all had combined to defeat the sight-seeing. Most of them were getting tired of the monotony of pasta in any of its varieties and sick, too, of tea with one tea bag per pot that was little more than hot water. Secretly they longed for their accustomed monotony of fried fish and chips or baked beans and good strong Indian tea well "mashed".

Mrs. Lawler and her friends, however, were in much better spirits. They had drunk their fill of the wonders of those picture galleries they had been able to visit and were all agreed that they must somehow manage a week in Florence in the off-season, when they could repeat and extend these pleasures.

Gwen Chilton too was in a cheerful mood. She had every reason to be so. Owen had met her again at the Ponte

Vecchio expressly to make amends for letting her get soaked in the thunderstorm. He had given her a fabulous coral necklace of the most delicately pink round beads of the stuff, quite a long one, too, costing the earth. She had worn it under her coat in the coach, not mentioning it to the others, but at lunch, when it lay there round her neck, glowing against the plain pale blue-grey of her straight tunic dress, it drew exclamations of surprise and admiration that made her blush and smile outwardly, while laughing immoderately inside. The poor old cats, she thought, as she explained that Owen had insisted on making her a present.

"He had a conscience, I suppose," she said. "For driving me down from the monastery in the car instead of letting me go in the coach where I should have been absolutely dry."

As if Owen ever had a conscience about anything, she told herself. Well, neither had she, for that matter. They had gone back to his hotel and she had rewarded him — and herself.

Rose, watching the flushed, pleased face of the little suitcase crook, as she now thought of Gwen, wondered grimly if this story was true, or if the girl had done a clever piece of shop lifting. Perhaps not, she considered, remembering the crowds on the Ponte Vecchio and the number of shop assistants on guard when she went into one of the jewellers to ask the price of a cameo and came out without it.

So Owen had funds, had he? Well, hadn't she known that, from the way he hired cars and so on. And appeared to be free to follow his fancy wherever it led. It galled her to see that it led to Gwen Chilton, but it could not be denied the girl was pretty and had a good — well, a really lovely figure. Perhaps if this infatuation showed signs of developing she might consider it her duty to warn him, tell him about the attempt on her luggage. No, that would

94

be fatal. Anyway she could never bring herself to tell tales. Just watch and perhaps warn Gwen.

"That girl seems to be making hay, doesn't she?" Myra said as the three sat with their coffee at the end of the meal.

"And the sun is shining again," said Flo. "No wonder she's feeling smug."

It was the first time Flo had shown bitterness. Remembering what Myra had told her about her friend, Rose said nothing. In a few minutes after that Billie called them to go to 'Roseanna'.

The rest of the drive to Venice was dull but the arrival there was not. On the contrary Rose Lawler found it fascinating. First the coach moved out along Mussolini's causeway that linked the mainland with the chief island of the Venice archipelago, the old Venice itself. From its arrival there the coach moved into a queue of cars and coaches waiting to be transported by car-ferry to the Lido, largest and most important of the outlying islands and the one that looked out over the Adriatic.

There was a considerable wait. In the end the passengers had to walk on to the ferry to lighten the coach in getting it aboard. After a voyage down the main channel, passing Venice itself, they crossed the seaway to the Lido, where the cars and coaches drive off and the tour got back into 'Roseanna' and were driven to their hotel.

"I thought there weren't any cars in Venice," Flo said to Billie, watching them drive past the coach before they started.

"There aren't," the courier answered. "There are no roads, only canals, on Venice itself. But there are roads on this island and it's quite a long one, though not very wide. You'll see. Besides it's the big bathing place, the very famous Lido . . ."

"I know. I know!" Flo told her. "Silly of me . . . I just thought — it just struck me . . ."

Billie smiled her professional smile and picked up her

loud speaker to announce their arrival, the usual hotel drill, the fact that they were free to make all their own arrangements for their stay in Venice, except for one tour to the very famous glass factory.

That evening Mrs. Lawler and her friends did no more than explore the tree-sheltered main street of shops and eating places, that ran the whole width of the island. With the leafy branches intertwined overhead along the pavements the whole effect was attractive in spite of the tourist crowds. The shade made it possible to walk in comfort while staying cool. Facing the shops, but on the edge of the wide pavement, small tables and chairs with awnings over swinging seats, invited the passers-by to refresh themselves.

"I'm not going to step further until I've had an ice," Flo declared, dropping into a chair at a vacant table to confirm her intention.

The others agreed. With the sun only beginning to sink, the deliciously cool air, the relief from those many hours of smooth but persistent movement on the road, they all three felt relaxed and happy. From time to time they noticed other members of the tour sauntering past, some staring fixedly at the shops, others looking about them and nodding and greeting when they recognised familiar faces. Gwen Chilton was not among them.

"I want to see the real sea," Rose said, finishing her ice and laying down the spoon.

"Of course," Myra agreed.

"I want another ice," Flo objected. "I'll stay here and you can pick me up on the way back."

The other two walked on, coming at last to the road that lay coast-wise along the length of the island. The sea however was still hidden by a thick, tall hedge of trees and bushes that screened it and the beach and the bathers from anyone in the road and from the cars that passed to and fro.

However, there were breaks in the screen, double gates,

drives-in, lodges where keepers took tickets and stored valuables and gave directions about huts.

"Very organised," Rose sighed, saddened and a little disgusted by all this. "Give me a good stretch of Devon or Cornish cove with a rock to undress behind and no one to interfere."

"And no one to warn the fools or pull them out when they go in at the wrong places and the wrong state of the tide," Myra added. "Come off it, Rose. This is, or used to be, a favoured playground of the wealthy. They must have expected continental comfort and safety. No one must drown, that would be unthinkable. No one must complain; that might lower the profits."

"We might book a hut for tomorrow afternoon," Rose said, changing the subject.

"We can do it at the hotel," Myra told her. "They have a strip of the beach and the huts with it. I asked."

"You know everything," Rose laughed.

When the three friends went down to breakfast the next morning Gwen was already seated at their table. She wore a serious face above a fresh pale yellow-flowered tunic and white slacks. No ornaments. The coral necklace was absent.

"You aren't wearing your corals," Rose said, as she took her place at the table.

Gwen did not answer.

"We're going over to San Marco," Myra began. "On one of the launches or whatever they're called. The one that stops everywhere, anyway. Will you be coming, Gwen?"

"I don't know," she said. "Yes, of course. But I don't know when."

She had eaten only half a roll and her coffee cup was half full, but she got up as she spoke and turned from the table.

"Your handbag!" Flo said to the girl's back.

Gwen turned quickly, swept up the bag and marched

away without a word, six inquisitive, astonished eyes following her as she threaded the tables and disappeared through the double swing doors.

Bloody snoopers, she told herself on her way to the lift. Nosy old cows! As if she'd go on sight-seeing with that lot! Sight-seeing! She'd had just about as much of that... If she'd only known what she was in for on this so-called tour... Except for meeting Owen... Owen... He could be sweet in spite of his funny face. He could send her as Jake never did now, never would again. After this job was finished she'd... well, what would she do? What *could* she do? Walk out, yes. But how...?

She waited in her room for the expected call. It came just after ten o'clock. A few minutes later, having put on the coral necklace and taken it off again because it clashed with the yellow tunic, really because she dared not say where she'd got it, she went out to take the next boat sailing over to Venice.

Five minutes after she had left the hotel the telephone in her room rang again. It went on ringing until the senior assistant at the reception asked the junior man whose room number he was trying to put the caller in touch with.

"The signora Chilton."

"Imbecile! She has gone out. Can't you see her key on the hook? Say to the caller Signora Chilton has gone out."

It was fun, Rose decided, to chug across the water to the various landing stages like a London bus moving from stop to stop. It was fun to see the contours of the famous old buildings change and shuffle as they altered their shapes and perspectives. Finally there was the excitement and awe of arriving beside the square itself, a beautifully different view of life from all those pictures and prints and illustrations and descriptions she had read and seen from time to time over the years.

The cathedral itself filled her with a greater sense of awe than any she had felt in Rome or Florence. She was in

98

no way a religious woman and had long ago abandoned the beliefs she had been taught in childhood and had held conventionally without much thought while she was working in Church of England schools. Since she had been ready to declare her agnosticism she had also not concealed her long established disgust and horror of the Rood. So it was an enormous relief and lightening of the spirit to find in the dark, gold-glittering interior of St. Mark's that eastern, Byzantine conception of Christ the over-looker, the judge, the all-wise, all-loving friend, the active son in human form of the Almighty Father, universal Good, Immortal God. No possibility here of false humanism, sentimental self-indulgent self-sacrifice.

Overcome by the surging of these thoughts that took her back over those events in her life that had first forced them to emerge, and at the same time moved by the sheer beauty and splendour of the gleaming intricate mosaics all about her, Mrs. Lawler walked slowly away from her companions. They did not follow her, for Myra especially remembered what she had heard, standing on the bridge above the Arno. Flo remembered the monastery of Monte Scenario and how familiar Rose had seemed with the rather doubtful Mr. Strong. There had been some trouble with Gwen, perhaps between that girl, would you call her trendy, and the strange man whose face gave her the creeps.

As Mrs. Lawler passed into the deep shadow of one of the solid pillars in the nave of the church, part of the shadow moved. Owen's hand touched her arm, closed on it, without any apparent effort checked her movement.

"I didn't see you, Owen," Rose said in a low voice.

"I didn't intend to be seen, except by you," he answered.

It was wickedly effective. In that place, in the mood it had imposed on her, the sheer sensual beauty she was accepting without northern puritan misgiving or southern superstition, laid her open to any guarded flattery from any quarter, not even allowing for this man's personal appeal in her most personal desire for atonement.

"Is anything the matter? Can I do anything?"

It was ridiculous, she thought humbly, at her age, but if only she could —

"Is it about Gwen?" she went on as he did not answer.

"Yes. How could you guess, Rose?"

"Tell me."

They still stood in the shadow of the pillar, where she tried to make out his face but could only really see the strong hand gripping her arm, sending its message of strength into her own body, together with its appeal, equally compelling.

"We were to meet, here in the cathedral, half an hour ago. She hasn't come. She isn't here."

"But she left the hotel before we did. I know, because I saw her key was up on the board as I left mine."

Quite definite, this. Because Mrs. Lawler always now put her key into the hand of the chief clerk at the desk and waited until he had disposed of it.

"It's very dark in here. Whereabouts were you to meet?"

"Just inside the door. Where they sell postcards."

"She wasn't there when we came in. Shall I go and look again? I could ask Myra and Flo. They're about somewhere."

"They've gone to see the picture behind the screen."

So he had been watching with the definite intention of speaking to her, but not to them? Again Rose felt, as she was meant to feel, the glow of being chosen, of being singled out, favoured. Poor Owen, so mistakenly in pursuit of such a worthless quarry. Never mind, if that was what he wanted.

"Have you tried the square?" she asked. "I don't think Gwen would find much in here to interest her, do you?"

A quick flare of anger took his hand from her arm, but he controlled it. What had he found himself or even looked for, except darkness, he raged inwardly? Aloud he said

100

in a very reasonable voice, "The square — yes. Come with me, Rose. Look a fool if I appear to be chasing..."

He gave a little embarrased laugh. Rose joined him. She had never felt so much pure pity, such sympathy, for this poor war victim. If Gwen had let him down already, even after accepting his truly magnificent present, well, it would be better sooner than later.

They moved to a side door, Owen showing the way. She did not consider that this was not the obvious way to find a waiting friend. But it provided a little more temporary shade for which she was grateful, as the sun was now high, the crowds very dense, mostly clustered below the clock tower with its two immense iron figures built with their hammers to beat out the hour upon the bell between them.

"They must be huge," Rose said gaily, forgetting Gwen, "the people up there on the tower beside them are tiny!"

He did not answer but took her arm again to urge her forward. Together, as an obvious tourist couple, they made their way through the surging mob.

It was Mrs. Lawler who saw Gwen first. She recognised the yellow tunic and the white slacks.

"There she is!" she said, pointing. "Over by the rows of chairs! On the sunny side! With — I don't recognise — I don't think it's any of our lot... Gwen!" she called, but they were a long way off and she couldn't be sure she had heard. Perhaps it wasn't Gwen after all. She tried again.

"Gwen!"

The girl turned, not looking directly at her, rather searching the crowd beyond and behind her. But Mrs. Lawler stopped dead, halted by that wild, chalk-white face. Gwen Chilton indeed, but in an extremity of fear. The man beside her turned away, the two men with him following. Gwen turned also, stumbling as she tried to catch up with them.

"It *was* Gwen!" Rose exclaimed, turning to Owen.

But Owen had vanished.

101

Chapter X

"OH THERE YOU ARE!" Myra was breathless.

"We waited at the main door for simply ages," Flo complained, breathing hard but not actually panting.

"I came out by the side door," Rose answered, still searching the crowd behind her for a sight of Owen, but not finding any. Gwen, too, when she turned her head the other way again, had disappeared, together with her escort of three strangers.

"Why? Why a side door, Rose? Why here? What's happened?" Myra persisted, at last finding her friend's eyes staring into hers with a very strange expression of both confusion and alarm.

"I don't think anything has actually *happened*," Rose said, slowly. "But I think a lot of things may be *going* to happen. Only I haven't the foggiest idea what."

"Honestly!" Flo was annoyed. "I'm for a good long sit-down and a coffee."

"Iced," Myra added. "And with music. Real music. They have orchestras at the cafés or just outside them."

"In the shade, then," Rose said, coming to herself with an effort. "The sun glares even through my sunglasses, after the blessed, heavenly, gloom inside." She smiled back at St. Mark's as she spoke, remembering Owen's voice, compelling, appealing.

It was so comfortable, so pleasing, so restoring, to listen

to heavenly Mozart while watching the crowds from a necessary distance that Mrs. Lawler decided not to confuse the minds of her friends with the problem of Owen's troubles and hesitations, the puzzle of his sudden departure. Instead she explained her recent behaviour by saying, "Didn't you see Gwen? Across the Square? That was what brought me up short. Just before you caught up with me."

"I thought it was Mr. Strong who stopped you?" Flo said.

"Mr. Strong?" So they had seen him.

"Yes. I noticed him first. Then he turned and went away."

"Did he? Which way?"

"Towards the shops. That first little street out of the Square."

"I saw Gwen," Myra said. "And I didn't see Mr. Strong. I must say I didn't think much of Gwen's new friends. Distinctly sinister."

"That was what I thought," Rose said, trying to make the remark light-heartedly. "Did you see her face? I think she knew them, but wasn't very pleased to see them here."

"Which doesn't surprise me," Myra answered. "No, I didn't see her face. I was focussing on the men. Villain with bodyguards. Heroine in ambush."

"I think you may be right at that." Rose gave up her pretended gaiety. Heroine in ambush. Then could one add, Hero evades it?

Flo's excited voice said, "Oh look, both of you! Straight across the Square, that boy with a guitar slung across his shoulders. The girl with him, long skirt and fringy leather waistcoat. Penny Banks, surely? Isn't it Penny Banks?"

"Yes," said Rose. "You're quite right. Penny. Not deported. Not in the nick. How very extraordinary."

Myra had left her chair and was threading her way past the tables. Her progress was slow, but from time to time she raised an arm and Rose was amused to see Penny first drag her partner round to face the ranks of chairs and then pull his arm up with her own to signal recognition in his turn.

"They're coming over," Flo said, with some surprise. "I had no idea she ever even noticed our existence."

"She noticed, but didn't acknowledge," Rose explained. "So now I very much doubt... Ah yes, Mr. and Mrs. Banks on our right. About twenty yards away. Yes, Penny's turning off a bit now. I hope Myra realises..."

The latter did, in time to turn to her friends and signal to them that she had been disappointed, had made a mistake.

"That mannerless child pretends she hasn't seen us either," Flo said, as the pair drew nearer with Myra returning, not many tables away.

Rose nodded and then smiled across the tables to Mrs. Banks, who returned the greeting. Mr. Banks, who was watching his daughter, stood up as she arrived at their table and sat down when she took her seat, leaving her to introduce her escort and the boy to find himself a chair. He dragged up two, one for himself and one for the guitar. An elderly waiter, approaching for orders, nearly tripped over the legs of this unorthodox accessory, swore at it, pulled it away. The guitar slid towards the ground but was saved just in time.

"Sock him one!" Penny said fiercely.

"Don't you dare!" Mr. Banks ordered, swivelling to speak to the waiter, at the same time pushing out a leg to intercept the young man.

"Belt up," the latter said to Penny.

The waiter moved the extra chair to its former place.

Though the music and the distant hum of the crowd prevented these exchanges from reaching the three friends, they understood what they saw and deplored it.

"Poor Mrs. Banks," Myra said. "She's so hopeless where Penny is concerned. Since the girl left us she's been so much more relaxed and chatty, hasn't she?"

"The knitting has put on a yard or two — if that's a good thing," Rose said.

"What I want to know," Flo sighed, "is what really happened to Penny. She certainly went away from the hotel in an ambulance. Was that really appendicitis or an overdose? Then she was supposed to have gone back to England to convalesce. But rumour said she'd been put on a charge, without bail. All nonsense, the lot of it. So what really ...?"

"Not our business," Myra told her firmly.

"I know it isn't." Flo was indignant. "If they were an ordinary nice family I wouldn't try to find out. But the parents are so dim and the girl's such a stinker — and now that insolent young man — Penny's breed, whoever he is."

"Come along," Rose said, getting up and beginning to move away. "I want to see the shops and the little canals and the gondolas at work. If there are any at work. That stack of them near our landing place made me think of the few hansom cabs in Trafalgar Square in the twenties when I was a child. Waiting. Waiting. On show, poor things. A sort of Victorian dinosaur."

That made them laugh and follow her willingly. So she walked on ahead, staring into shop windows, crossing narrow bridges, pausing to take photographs of picturesque corners where the dark water reflected sunlit old houses standing up from it, sunk now to the bottoms of their green-slimed doors. Everywhere she saw new and unexpected sights and marvelled at what she saw; everywhere she looked for Owen, but did not find him.

At last they came to the Rialto and stood there gazing at the actual, the living Canaletto spread below them. The morning was nearly over. It was time to go back to the hotel on the Lido.

"Don't forget we have booked a hut on the beach," Myra reminded her friends.

"Then we must get a boat from here," Flo decided.

"And we can take photographs as we go down this . . . this . . ."

"Grand Canal," Rose supplied as she set off briskly down the steps from the bridge.

At the San Marco stopping place Mr. and Mrs. Banks joined their ferry, but alone now. The couple looked sad, but brightened when they saw the three friends and made their way slowly but patiently through the intervening crowd until they reached them, when Mrs. Lawler moved to make room for Mrs. Banks on the seat beside her, while Mr. Banks leaned over the back of it to join in their conversation.

As usual the couple were prepared to compare notes about their sightseeing that morning, their opinions of what they had seen, their plans for the rest of the day.

"We're going to bathe," Rose told them.

"Well, I don't know about bathing," Mrs. Banks said. "But we've booked a place on the beach. Only they said we might have to share the hut with others."

"They said that to us too. I think they say it to anyone, so as not to disappoint the customers."

Mrs. Banks, listening, nodded.

So Rose was not surprised when they arrived at their hut that afternoon to find the Banks pair already settled in two long chairs in the sun, Mr. Banks in bathing trunks and linen sun hat and dark glasses, his wife in her usual flowered nylon summer dress, no hat, no glasses, but her knitting flowing over her lap on to the sand.

The three joined them, greeted them with pleasure and surprise at not finding strangers in possession. Mr. Banks smiled up at them.

"My doing," he explained. "Glad to see you approve."

"Of course we do," Myra told him. "We'll just change and join you in the sea, if you're thinking of going in."

"Thinking, yes. Too darned lazy, though."

"Nonsense," said Flo stoutly, making for the hut.

They all changed and Mr. Banks was moved to give his

106

chair to Rose, who said she would let her lunch settle for a bit longer.

"Are you not going in?" she asked Mrs. Banks as she sat down.

"I never bathe," was the answer. "They tried to teach me to swim at school, but I was too scared to take my feet off the bottom even with someone holding me by the back of my costume. Do you swim, Mrs. Lawler?"

"Oh yes, I have always swum," she answered, smiling.

As long as she could remember. Well, yes, though she remembered best those Olympics, just before the War, when she had been hailed as the girl champion swimmer, near champion, no medal but promise of one, what would now be called a "teenage wonder" or some such nonsense. At sixteen, rising seventeen.

"I still do swim — when the water's warm, as I suppose it must be here."

She waited a few minutes and then said, "We saw Penny was back. You don't mind my asking about her, do you? We were so sorry she had to leave the tour."

"No, you weren't," said Mrs. Banks. It was the first definite, the first strong statement Mrs. Banks had ever made and it quite startled Rose, who sat up straight and said, in a voice to match, "Well, in a way we were all glad to lose the tantrums and so on. We were sorry for you and Mr. Banks."

"Which didn't stop a lot of you making up stories about Penny. You needn't think we didn't hear them, in a round-about way, of course."

"Stories, yes," said Rose. "To be perfectly honest, we three did discuss what could have happened, but we never passed on anything or discussed it with anyone else, I do assure you. So I meant it when I said we were glad to see Penny looking well and strong in Venice this morning."

"Very well," said Mrs. Banks, relapsing into her familiar soft, vague manner. "Penny had a sudden acute appendix, they thought at the hospital, not typhoid as the local doctor thought. We asked Billie to announce it to the tour, only I don't believe she did it properly. She went to hospital in an ambulance from the hotel. Oh, I know there were rumours of a police ambulance and drugs and I don't know what all."

She paused, staring at Rose, who stared back, making no answer.

"She left hospital and we arranged for her to go to my sister in Wimbledon to convalesce. We asked Billie to announce this also and again she did it too vaguely. So of course the rumours started that she had been moved to prison on a charge of having drugs in her possession. All false."

Again Mrs. Banks paused and again Mrs. Lawler waited.

"But Penny, being so independent and — and wilful . . ." Mrs. Banks' voice wavered, but she continued to knit vigorously.

"Came back from Wimbledon?" asked Rose gently.

"Yes. With Gary. That's her boy-friend. Her latest boy-friend. Of course we cancelled her booking when she left the tour, but they hadn't filled it, they couldn't, could they, halfway through? She's at liberty to use the booked room here and the two other separate one night stops on the way back to Genoa."

"Will she? I mean what about the boy-friend?"

"I don't know if she will. They joined us for coffee in the Square, as you noticed. But they didn't come over with us to the Lido."

"Or turn up for lunch, either. I don't think the rest of the tour know she's back. Only Billie, I suppose."

"I've left all that to my husband," Mrs. Banks said with a glance seawards, where the stout figure was threshing about between the long waves, with Myra and Flo jumping and splashing beside him.

"I think I'd better go and join them," Rose said. "I'm sorry we have all been so lacking in . . . understanding and

—and just commonsense. Too much melodrama in the newspapers and on the goggle-box, I'm afraid."

Mrs. Banks graciously inclined her head. Poor woman, Rose thought, marching away across the sand; ivory from the neck up. As for Penny, if that vicious little piece was not smoking reefers in the coach why was all that mixed bag of noses so certain of the smell wafted back to them?

The sea, three lazily foaming waves of it above a bed of sand, welcomed her with cool pleasure as she dropped into it. No horrid icy shock, no dragging undertow, no decision to make about possible off-shore, on-shore, across-shore currents. Perhaps too shallow for continued pleasure, she decided, when she found her feet, even her knees, meeting the bottom as she tried to swim. She stood up to wade out to the others and when she caught up with them found all three only a little more than waist deep, watching her.

"Isn't it lovely?" they called.

"Gorgeous," she shouted, turning to lie on her back and splash before rolling over and trying to swim down under the water to Flo's legs. The action failed for want of depth.

"Is there no more water further out?" she appealed to Mr. Banks, who was also watching her.

"According to the notice, plenty," he said. "For strong swimmers only. Beware, beware!"

"Like that, is it? I see."

She lay on her back again, turning her head away from the direct eye of the sun. The hard line of the horizon blurred beyond the edge of the beach, while the sky there showed a row of little white clouds, faint, fluffy, merging with the sea.

Land again, she told herself. Yugoslavia, of course. Some day when she had saved up again, she would come back to Venice and take ship down that far coast to Dubrovnik and on and on to Corfu . . .

"I'm going in now," Myra called.

"I'm staying," she called back, too contented to say more. When she stood up again she found she was alone, so she started to swim seawards until she found she had passed the last warning notice. At this she turned back, not wishing to bring life-savers from their lair, wherever that might be.

Gwen Chilton appeared at dinner that evening. She was early, in fact already drinking her usual pink apéritif in the bar when Rose and the others joined her.

Mrs. Lawler decided there was no point in pretending not to have seen her. She no longer showed white-faced fear. On the contrary she looked both happy and relaxed, her smooth skin the faintly pink bronze the older women so much admired.

"I saw you in the Square this morning," Rose said, going up to the girl. "With new friends, or are they old ones?"

Gwen only smiled, so Mrs. Lawler went on. "I had just come out of the cathedral. With Owen Strong, actually. I came across him inside. He was waiting for you, I suspect."

She said this with some degree of archness, for which she cursed herself for an old fool. She expected a laugh in reply, together with a denial, a blush perhaps.

She got none of these. Gwen, who had half risen at the sound of Owen's name, was now sunk back in her chair, chalk-faced again, eyes closed, a little shuddering moan escaping from her slack mouth.

Chapter XI

THESE MANIFESTATIONS, GENUINE though they were this time, aroused no alarm still less any sympathy, in her companions. Instead, at a silent signal from Mrs. Lawler, they all three crept away to Myra's room to discuss Gwen's latest display of temperament in private.

So when the girl opened her eyes, instead of the usual ring of embarrassed faces she found that she was alone. Not even a single member of the tour, those she generally had a few words with, those who merely exchanged a "good night" or "good morning", those who avoided doing so; not even Billie or Mario, the driver, both of whom usually dined with the tour group and often had local friends in each place of call; not even these symbols of protection were within sight.

Gwen sat and shivered inwardly. She might have known what would happen from Jake's response to her last two telephone calls. But she did not expect to see him so soon. It had been a complete surprise, a horrifying surprise, to see his tall figure, his dark face, black hair, black eyes, blue chin except for that nasty little pointed black beard he now wore, surging towards her from the entrance to the Doge's Palace as she was making a cautious approach to St. Mark's where she had promised to meet Owen.

Jake had swept her away into the middle of the Square under the scorching sun, where his friends, his bodyguard,

111

had greeted her with carefully veiled, sneering smiles, sending more waves of alarm through her as they closed in, one just behind Jake, the other just behind herself.

"I thought . . ." she had stammered. "I didn't expect . . ."

"You thought because you'd had no trouble with the Law here and none from home or from . . ."

"I tried to explain when I called you," she interrupted desperately. "The tour is still O.K. The cover couldn't be better, really. This Mrs. Lawler . . ."

"Never mind her," Jake had broken in roughly. "She's negligible. Who's this feller you say keeps following . . ."

Again she interrupted, because she could not bear to have him drag out the truth about Owen. Which he could do, would do for certain, if he set his wicked mind to it, his mean, evil, trouble-seeking, cunning, grasping . . .

"Oh Jake!" she gasped, clutching his arm. She looked about her for a way of escape and found it. "Oh Jake, look behind me. A tall, thin old limey woman, staring at us. She's always like that; Mrs. Lawler. I told you. I told you. Following me like a hawk. Nuts, I shouldn't wonder. Never remarks on it, never asks questions . . ."

"Never mind her," Jake had repeated. "You give me what I want. This other pest. What's he like? What's he want, for God's sake, beside the usual, which you've probably given, so what else? Come on — spill!"

In despair, in bitter fear, she had denied unfaithfulness, denied betrayal, denied blackmail. How could the stranger try that on when he didn't even know she had any secrets worth disclosing. She denied everything of relevance in fact about Owen, so that in the end Jake had said, "It's no good, honey, trying to put across it's your fascination on its own that's sending this guy. When I first made you, could be so. You were sure thing a raving beauty. But that's eleven, twelve year back. Never now. Never no more."

It had been a good opportunity to end the bullying with outraged tears and to get away back to the hotel. But in the siesta time, when she had avoided the expedition to

112

the beach and had gone out to find a cool shade among the luxuriant bushes in the hotel garden, her peace, that was no true peace but a desperate search for a means of escape from her dual predicament, was broken suddenly and her mind thrown into fresh confusion by the appearance of Owen himself.

Dressed in a worn, but clean beige-coloured linen suit, he dropped into a chair beside her and said calmly, but with a steely look in his grey eyes, "That was Jake, I suppose?"

"Yes," she answered sullenly, to gain time.

"You sent for him?"

"No one *sends* for Jake."

"Asked then?"

"No."

It was no good trying to hold him off, she knew. In his way he was every bit as bad as Jake. If not worse. When Jake really blew his top she could expect a blow at least, a bullet at worst. Violence, anyway, strong enough to hurt, meant to hurt. But over quickly, whichever it was. With Owen it never showed, except by this everlasting persistence and behind it a threat, never yet spoken, but always to be feared.

So now she turned her head to look him straight in the eyes, hoping to impress him that he was getting the real truth at last. She saw no other way.

"You may as well have it straight," she said. "It's been Jake all along, of course. And he isn't — wasn't — my husband. We've been together for years and I haven't been the only one by a long chalk. He isn't the English business man I told you. I haven't run off with his business takings. He hasn't got a business at all, not the sort of business I pretended he had. I met him in the States and started — well, working for him there. I don't even know his real nationality. He has a lot of passports, that I do know."

"And speaks a lot of languages?"

113

"How did you guess?"

Owen ignored this. He was wondering how much of the latest story he could believe. Gwen was incapable of speaking the plain truth about anything. But on the whole there did not seem much point in discounting the facts. She was a less than willing tool, it seemed, of the brutal, ruthless American crook. She had been sent to Switzerland with a load of lolly to deposit, then to England to pick up this two-week tour in Italy. The plan must have been for her to remain with the tour until she got back to Gatwick. Then Jake would join her, they would fly out to Geneva, she as his Swiss wife, visit the bank, retrieve the spoil and Bob's your uncle.

But why that heavy suitcase? Why not a much less ostentatious method of stashing away stolen gains? Was it indeed money? Why not jewels, bullion, pictures, carefully packed ceramics, priceless old coins?

He tried to remember the recent disappearances of precious objects but could remember nothing suitable.

"How did you guess?" Gwen repeated.

Again he ignored the question. Instead he reached for her hand and began to stroke it and then the arm to which it belonged, brown, rounded, bare to the shoulder. She pulled her hand away but the eyes that continued to search his were now troubled.

"You've got to give up, Owen," she began. "You can't take on Jake. You daren't. I daren't let you. I've stalled so far, but he'll have it out of me in the end. I know him. I think he's part Italian."

"Mafia, eh?" said Owen, smiling for the first time since he had found her in the garden.

"I wouldn't know. All I do know is you've got to get out. Now. Today. Before he finds out you've — we've ..."

She shuddered, hugging herself as if a cold wind had just blown over her.

Owen made up his mind.

"I'll go," he said firmly. "Now don't get excited. Wait

114

for it. I'll go, but on condition you go with me. And that we go straight to Geneva and pick up whatever it was you deposited there and then we'll disappear without trace."

"*You must be mad!*" She was half out of her seat before Owen checked her. But she felt as she had once before done, that his grip, though not as violent as Jake's would have been, was many times stronger. And Owen was not even angry. His quiet voice was continuing.

"It would not be madness," he was saying. "On the contrary the only sensible thing in the circumstances. You are the one who put the lolly in safe deposit. Yes? So it is you who must get it out. You have a Swiss name and a Swiss passport in that name. We withdraw what we can use from that safe deposit and — as I said before — disappear till the heat is off."

"It would be on from Jake and he never lets up, I can tell you."

He saw that she was wishing inwardly he might be right; that she might escape from her servitude. Poor little camp dolly; it would be quite a change to have her all to himself for a bit. Not for good. Compulsive liars were too dangerous. But money for jam . . ."

"You're scared," he taunted.

"Bloody scared! So would you be if you knew Jake as I do."

Gwen was getting upset. Between these two men, these two crooks, she was being tossed about till she didn't know if she was on her head or her heels. And no one, repeat no one, to advise her. The three old girls who had seemed so willing to support her in the early days of the trip would be horrified to learn the whole truth. Besides, they'd advise her to go to the police, carabinieri! No, thank you. Besides, whatever it was in that Swiss bank, she'd taken the risk in putting it in, as usual, and she'd like to see a bit of it for herself, really for herself, not just in the shape of what Jake called "a ball", night clubs, clothes and that.

115

"We ought to leave tomorrow night, if I can fix it," Owen said smoothly. "Your tour moves on the day after."

"To Verona," she answered, deliberately not answering his proposal.

"I'll be back," he said and was gone before she could protest she had not decided, had not at all made up her mind.

Owen had left his Venice contact at a café with a bar open to the street and chairs and tables in a small enclosure of clipped oleander bushes of the kind that divided the two sides of the autostrada behind strong metal barriers. It was most suitably secluded from passers-by, while the hum of their voices and the noise of traffic in the road made low-voiced conversation safe from overhearing.

"Any luck?" Owen asked.

"Fair enough, Mr. Strong. Sorry — Mr. Culver."

Owen frowned. When had he slipped up? This failed photographer had always known him as Culver. That was the name he'd used at the garage in Florence where he'd abandoned the long black car and thought, when he hired the yellow job, that they would arrange for the other to be sent back to Nice, complete with its log book and hire papers.

"Culver," he said, putting a little menace into his voice. "Culver, Tito, and don't get confused. O.K.?"

"O.K." said the photographer, swallowing hard, his eyes flickering.

"You'll bring this new car over here tomorrow morning, hired in the name of Culver, papers all correct. And you'll take the other back to Florence. Here are the papers and the key. You'll pay for it in cash, that I'll give you tomorrow when you bring me the new key and papers, O.K.?"

"O.K." repeated the other, breathing more easily.

Owen explained a few more details of his plans for the future, after which the two men left the shelter of the oleander hedge. Tito moved off to the quayside to take a

116

vaporetto back to Venice, while Owen, a few minutes later, sauntered away towards the Lido beach.

Earlier that day he had rung up the tour hotel to book a room for two nights and having secured it had packed his suitcase and travelled across the water with it. He had just left the case in his new quarters when he caught sight of Gwen in the garden.

Walking out now to the beach he checked his identity and new address with the attendant at the gate and walked down to the sand, looking about him for familiar faces.

Paper currency or hard cash, that was what he needed, what he must have within the next twelve hours, if his plans were to work out as he intended. But his credit was low at the moment, thanks to that article in the Rome paper about the car he'd hired in Nice from that hitherto reliable friend, Bertrand. A shame, because Bertrand had tempted him to take the thing, a real beauty incidentally, at a very low rental, provided he drove it successfully to its next destination in Naples for private export to Tangier. Which he had done, but Naples wouldn't take delivery, so back to Rome, where he'd read the article and Rollo had not been able to help him unload the thing. So on to Florence and a bit of luck in the shape of a thunderstorm and a very carefully, very slightly bent garage. But expensive. Too damned expensive.

He moved at a leisurely walk along the soft sand, searching in his practised way without attracting any attention to himself. At one point he saw in the distance the tall figure of Mrs. Lawler going down towards the sea and two figures among the waves beckoning to her.

Mrs. Lawler? No. He could engage her sympathy, ask for advice, even help, but never for money. He knew that sort. On to the least hint of a touch, she'd freeze. Very sorry, quite impossible. No, don't apologise, we'll just forget it. Surely the British Consul . . . A pain in the neck, the old bitch. All old bitches.

He saw a waving hand and with an answering wave

moved towards it. The medical pair, Gwen called them. What were the names? Yes, fat jolly Mrs. Franks and her niece, starchy Miss Hurry.

He sank on to the sand beside the stout one, because she had pulled her deck chair into the shade of the hut. Miss Hurry, in a neat costume — no bikini for her, thank you very much — had stretched her very attractive body in the sun: she turned a lazy head as Owen joined them and rolled over on to her back. All women are the same, he thought. Must have their tits admired. He smiled at her to show his admiration. Mrs. Franks giggled.

"Any more of you on the beach?" he asked. "I came down on the off chance."

"Of seeing Gwen Chilton, I suppose?" said Mrs. Franks, archly. "She's not here."

"Oh well," he said carelessly. "But you two are."

"And the schoolmarms, as we call them. Out there in the sea."

"So they are."

"And the Bankses."

"Really?"

"Not Penny. The daughter, you know. But several of us saw her on the Square at St. Mark's this morning. With a long-haired boy."

"And a guitar," Miss Hurry added.

Owen expressed surprise.

"Yes. We didn't expect it. She was supposed to have gone back home when she left hospital."

"To convalesce," Miss Hurry again filled out her aunt's remark.

"Oh yes," Owen said. "Wasn't she whisked off in an ambulance as an emergency? I heard a rumour she'd been in trouble over a drug, but I didn't believe it."

"She'd be capable of any vice," Miss Hurry said severely.

"Oh, come now!" He guessed from their manner, the pair of them, some mystery about the case of Miss Banks.

118

Promising — perhaps. He went on, "Gwen told me it was an acute appendix. Was that just another rumour?"

"You could call it that," Mrs. Franks said slowly.

"Aunt! Careful!"

The warning was unmistakable.

Owen said seriously, "Of course you two ladies are both medicos, hospital nurses, I believe. Am I right? Well, then, it would be strange if Miss Banks herself or her mother had not asked one or other of you when she began to feel ill. Herself even, before her mother."

Mrs. Franks said, "Her mother would be the last person she was likely to talk to."

"She is a very wild, unprincipled girl, Mr. Strong," Miss Hurry told him. She was sitting up now, showing every reluctance to taking this conversation further.

"My fault, nurse," Owen said. "I do know that, at least. I was just curious. About the possibility of it being a drug case. So appallingly common these days. I won't ask any more questions. Obviously the poor girl was ill and she appealed to you or your aunt for help, knowing she would get it and your discretion, too."

"I wasn't going to help her," Miss Hurry said frankly. "Except to tell her she'd have to go into hospital."

"I was sorry for her and I don't mind saying so," the older woman said in spite of her niece's effort to stop her. "You don't have forty years' experience as a fully qualified midwife, as I did, without learning that a bit of sympathy and tolerance don't do anyone in this world any harm and sometimes prevents a tragedy."

Miss Hurry turned back on to her face, ashamed of her aunt's garrulous give-away. But Mr. Strong hardly seemed to have heard it. He was already talking about the view and the little sailing boats moving about in the light breeze beyond the bathers. He said a few words about two of the three older women as they left the sea and walked back up the beach. He noticed Mr. Banks join them and Mrs. Lawler turn to swim or wade farther out.

119

Chapter XII

OWEN STAYED TALKING to the nurses for nearly half an hour after he had coaxed that potential gold nugget from the fat old midwife.

So now he knew for sure — well, pretty nearly for sure — why Penny had been rushed off to hospital. An abortion, of course, begun illegally and inexpertly, as so often in former times in England. Odd no one seemed to have thought of the possibility except these two professionals. They were all so conditioned to drugs being the natural feature of the hippy complex. Freak clothes, long hair, bad manners, sullen temper, violent response to criticism, they'd seen it all displayed by Penelope Banks, the silly twit. So they must pin on crime as well. Even he, himself, had been ready to believe she'd been shipped off inside, not to hospital at all.

While he continued to chat with Mrs. Franks his busy mind darted from one place to another. A fat lot of good to move into the tour hotel; to settle with Gwen to leave for Geneva the following night; to order Tito to rustle up a car and have it in the park ready for the ferry not later than tomorrow afternoon and then find he hadn't enough dough to settle with the poor chap. Not to speak of the journey, petrol, food, servicing, and again petrol. So that interview with Dad Banks, that crucial interview, must be arranged *and must succeed*, by nightfall that day, no later.

Even nightfall might be too late if it meant clearing with a bank ... So ...

"I can see Mrs. Lawler in the sea and her friends walking back," he said, pointing to where she and Mr. Banks still wallowed in the waves, "But I don't see Gwen. No, you said she hadn't come."

"That's right."

"And there's Mr. Banks, isn't it? But not Mrs. B."

"She doesn't bathe," Miss Hurry said. "They were talking about it at lunch. Penny hadn't turned up for lunch. I think she stayed in Venice with the boy-friend. Mr. Banks wanted a swim, so he said he'd come down. I don't think she ever goes in."

"No, she doesn't," Mrs. Franks added. "She told me she never goes in, her circulation won't stand it."

"You mean she gets too cold?"

"I suppose so. It's a common excuse for not learning to swim, isn't it?"

"I wouldn't know," Owen told her, losing patience.

He watched Mr. Banks come back up the beach, he watched Mrs. Lawler swim out a fair distance and then come in. He waited until he saw Rose Lawler and her friends, changed into their summer dresses, so correct, so dull, go past behind the huts towards the gate into the road. Then he said goodbye to the nurses and moved away.

He moved slowly, searching among the nearby huts for his marked quarry. At first he thought the nurses had let him down, but presently he caught sight of Mrs. Banks, or rather of her knitting, borne before her as she emerged from the fourth of the hotel's reserved huts. He stopped to help her out over the step and as he did so glanced inside. A pile of masculine clothes lay at one side of a bench running round three sides of the little building, with hooks in the walls above the bench.

"I thought I saw Mr. Banks beginning to walk up from the sea," he said, guiding her to a long chair on the sand.

"I wouldn't wonder," she answered. She gave a quick

121

glance seaward before unrolling her knitting. Owen, who had just had a promising idea, went on. "I came along with that intention myself, but they wouldn't hire me a towel at the gate."

"They don't," Mrs. Banks said. "Nor costumes."

"Oh, I've got trunks with me," he explained. "I just thought I need not bother to carry a towel down and take it back wet."

She did not answer, knitting steadily.

"You don't mind if I change in your hut?" he asked.

"Of course not. All these five belong to the hotel, I think. Mrs. Lawler and her friends were here but they've gone back. Reg decided to have a second dip. He came up to tell me."

Owen went in to the hut and came out very soon, leaving his own clothes on the bench at a little distance from those of Mr. Banks.

"I've just been talking to Mrs. Franks and Miss Hurry," he said. "They thought I might find you and Mr. Banks. But not Penny."

"Not — *what*?"

"They said Penny must have stayed over in Venice with the boy-friend, instead of coming back to lunch."

Put like that, with a suggestion of something not quite discreet about Penny's behaviour set Mrs. Banks to rolling up the knitting and struggling to her feet.

"I think I'll go and talk to them," she said.

When she had gone Owen gave his short, silent laugh as he walked briskly to the sea. He pushed his way through the first wave, dived neatly through the next and came up, as he intended, about ten yards from Mr. Banks. He flung back his rather thin but shortish hair and said heartily, "Hullo, there!"

"Hullo!" said Mr. Banks. He had been too far off and much too preoccupied with his bathing to notice Strong's arrival, nor was he particularly pleased to see the fellow, whom he still vaguely distrusted.

"Marvellous, isn't it?" Owen said, allowing himself to sink on to his back so that he could float while looking about him. But the water was too shallow and the third wave broke over him so that he emerged spluttering and laughing, but inwardly raging. Mr. Banks, he saw, had begun to move towards the shore.

It looked as if he had done this deliberately as an avoiding action. So much the worse for him if he was going to make the touch more difficult, Owen promised himself. But he decided not to cut short his own bathe. Banks did not know yet that they were sharing the same hut, but he would find that out from his wife if she had gone back there from her visit to the two nurses.

He watched Mr. Banks' progress to the beach, stepping high, pushed forcibly forward when a wave struck him in the back, but making steady progress. His speed increased when he reached the sand. It became difficult to distinguish him from the crowd of beach walkers, games players, child minders and so on. But persevering Owen was able to pick out his intended victim again as soon as he reached the prostrate forms of the sunbathers near the huts. Was that Mrs. Banks in the long chair where he had himself ensconced her? Too far away to be certain. Too far away to see if any of the figures near that hut was knitting. Too far away, but too soon to go out himself. Give Banks time to dress first.

Lazily Owen waded further off-shore. He was not a strong swimmer, nor an elegant one. He could put on a show of the modern crawl for a few strokes at a time, but he soon reverted to the simple froglike breast stroke he had learned as a boy. Nevertheless he managed, part swimming, part walking, to reach the official limit of the swimming area and stood up, the water now shoulder high, to look first at the beach where he could no longer distinguish one hut from another and then out to sea.

The small sailing boats he had noticed when he first walked down to the water were still there and seemed to be about the same distance away. They did not appear to have made much progress towards Trieste where he had thought before they might be heading. It was difficult to assess their size, so far off. But there was a new feature now, a white motor launch, at first moving across the seascape at about the level of the yachts, then altering course to drive straight for the beach.

Straight for me, thought Owen, if the fools don't alter course again, as they must, as they surely must. He began to swim again, uncomfortably aware that he had gone out farther than any other bather, that he was a particularly slow swimmer and that the noise of the launch's engines was growing louder every second.

He did not want to stop swimming, to show his incompetence, but he knew he was getting into shallower water and so the pursuing boat, if it was really pursuing, must soon turn off to avoid going aground. So he stopped his desperate floundering attempt at speed, let his feet sink, found the sand sooner than he expected and faced about, with his hands up to his eyes to sweep away the water, but his small cold eyes peeping through the gaps between his fingers.

The launch was indeed just turning away. It was sideways on now, apparently all set to move to the narrow pier that stuck out to sea from the end of the private part of the beach some distance along the coast.

But it was not the launch and its manoeuvres that sent a thrill of shock through Owen as he turned to swim again towards the beach. It was the clear view he had had of its occupants, who were the three that had sent him fading instantly from Mrs. Lawler's side at St. Mark's Square that morning.

Jake and Jake's bodyguard. The whole opposition, in fact. Why the launch? Why this patrol along the shore? Looking for Gwen, who had not joined the bathing party? Or looking for Gwen's friends? Where had Nurse Franks said they would be? Farther along the beach? Changed

124

their minds and gone sight-seeing? Unlikely. And Gwen? She'd have had time to leave the hotel garden and go to the quayside, only five minutes walk away, to join the launch. So was she in it? Had she recognised him? Told Jake, or simply kept out of sight? Was she reliable enough not to betray him? He doubted it.

Common sense told him to get out while the going was — not good — but still possible. But greed held him, linked with that possessive feeling, half attraction, half contempt, he still had for Gwen. He could not give her up, nor the hope of gain.

His mind was still in a turmoil of questions unanswered, perhaps unanswerable, when he finally arrived at the hut where Mrs. Banks sat knitting as before and Mr. Banks reclined on a rubber mattress, dressed only in a pair of white trousers, his broad chest exposed, sun-tan oil glistening from its sparse greying hairs.

Owen sat down on the sand near them. He had worn his bathing trunks under his trousers and now regretted he must dry off in the sun, having no towel. This process would not last very long, he hoped, because the second move he must take with the Banks couple depended upon his getting into his clothes before Reg Banks went into the hut again for his shirt and jacket.

The beach was too hot, the afternoon sun was still high overhead, so the drying business happily took no more than half an hour. At the end of this time, Owen got up to brush the damp sand from his seat and the backs of his thighs.

All this time he had chatted at intervals with Mrs. Banks, who responded without enthusiasm, but well within the bounds of good manners. Mr. Banks had volunteered little to the conversation, but enough to show that his eyes, behind his dark glasses, were not closed in sleep, but against the direct rays of the sun.

"I'll go in and dress now," Owen said, "Unless you want the hut, Banks."

"No, you go ahead," the latter grunted. But he rolled over and sat up on the rubber mattress, planting his feet on the sand beside it and supporting himself on his spread arms.

Owen went through the bare open outer part of the hut into the small cubicle behind it. Mr. Banks' clothes were in the same place as before, the same neat pile apart from the white trousers. His own pile was quite undisturbed. He must put them all on, he decided, then there could be no discussion about how they had appeared to Banks when he went in to dry himself and get into his trousers.

It did not take him more than a few minutes to dress. He had cigarettes in a packet in the side pocket of his jacket. He took one out, but did not light it. Nor did he put the garment on. Instead he moved his pocket diary into his hip pocket and his wallet that had been there into an inside breast pocket of the jacket. Now was the moment. Action.

Mrs. Banks was startled into dropping her knitting when Owen burst from the hut, wild-eyed, his jacket over one arm, his shirt unbuttoned.

"My wallet!" he gasped. "It's gone!"

"What's gone?" asked Mr. Banks, who had relapsed on to the mattress, this time face down.

"My wallet!" Owen dragged out his diary from his hip pocket. "This . . . look . . . it's my diary. Same sort of size. I didn't notice when I put on the bags. Same sort of feel — deliberate — must have been!"

By this time Mr. Banks had hoisted himself from the mattress and struggled to his feet.

"Are you saying you've been robbed of your wallet?" he said in a slow, accusing voice.

"Looks like it," Owen answered. He had put his jacket down on an empty deck chair while he lit his cigarette from a lighter he had taken from the same pocket as the packet of cigarettes. He now more calmly buttoned his shirt and put on the jacket. He patted the various pockets, pulling

126

out a handkerchief and refolding it, putting away the diary he had pulled from his hip pocket. All the time he drew on the cigarette with every sign of internal dismay, surrounding himself with a little cloud that made him cough. He beat it away, whereupon it enveloped Mrs. Banks who coughed as well.

"Oh, *sorry*!" Owen said in a disturbed voice. "I do beg your pardon!"

"You've had your wallet *stolen*?" Mr. Banks repeated, less accusing now than astonished. "How on earth could anyone... Mildred's been sitting here the whole afternoon..."

"Not quite all of it," she said. "I did go along to talk to Mrs. Franks for a few minutes."

"Leaving the hut unguarded?"

"Well, I could see it from their hut."

"When was this?"

"Must have been after I arrived," Owen said. "I had a few words with the nurses on my way here. I saw several of the tour people and you, Banks, in the water. Mrs. Banks said I could shed my things in your hut, so I did and went off to the sea almost at once."

"Yes," she agreed. "After you'd gone I went along for a few minutes. It can't have been long, because you came out, Reg, not ten minutes after Mr. Strong went in and I was here again when you got back, wasn't I?"

"That's right."

They were all silent then, looking at one another with anxious, wary eyes.

"So whoever nicked my wallet, must have been on the prowl," Owen said. "Easy enough with the huts in a tight row, as they are. Nip in and out. Could be anyone... visitor, tourist even. They keep the general public out with their thick hedge and the gates and the gate keepers. But there must be a lot of casual staff, hut cleaners and that, you'd think."

"What will you do?" Mrs. Banks said. "Go to the police?"

"I'd much rather not. The wheels of the Law in this country grind very, very slowly."

"Was there much in your wallet?" Mr. Banks asked.

"Just my spending money and my traveller's cheques. In fact everything till the banks open tomorrow."

"But they'll . . ." began Mrs. Banks, but her husband checked her.

"I expect your hotel in Venice will fix you up," he said firmly. "I think we'd better get a move on, Mildred. I'll just get dressed. Excuse me, Mr. Strong."

Mrs. Banks rolled up her knitting. She made no further effort to talk. Nor did Owen. The touch had failed almost before it got going. That was plain enough. Ask his hotel, indeed. When he was now booked into the tour hotel in the name of Culver. Was that a mistake? No. Not really. Banks need never know. He did not propose to have any meals in the place. He had paid in advance for his room for the two nights he would use it. Reg Banks would get the full treatment in the morning. The very full treatment, he promised himself.

He laughed as he waved goodbye to the pair when they left him. He stretched himself out on Mrs. Banks's long chair, looked at his watch and decided he had nearly an hour left before he must meet Tito and take delivery of the new car.

Chapter XIII

WHEN OWEN HAD left her in the hotel garden Gwen waited there for another half-hour before setting off for Venice again. Since she went straight for the quayside she did not encounter any members of the tour. All the beach parties had long since reached the shore and Owen was with Tito, hidden behind the oleander hedge while everyone outside it was hidden from him.

Gwen was rather late in reaching the Square but Jake, sitting with his bodyguards on the shady side of it, did not reproach her. Instead he announced a treat for her.

"What's that?" she asked.

He got up before she had time to sit down.

"Come and see," he said.

They moved out of the Square to the waterside, passing the ranks of gently moving, moored gondolas and coming to three launches, white-painted, their brasses sparkling as they swung lazily at their moorings.

There they stopped. Jake gave an order, the bodyguards leaped on to the nearest vessel and while one of them dived below to attend to the engines, the other took hold of the stern warp to draw the boat in close to the quay. Jake stepped on board, handed Gwen over after him and took her with him to the wheelhouse. At a shout from below the man on deck stepped ashore, untied the warp near the bollard and with both strands held firmly jumped back on to the launch as the engines broke into a roar.

"Fend off!" Jake shouted from the wheelhouse. There were rubber tyres hanging on both sides of the launch. Being on the outside of the row, with a substantial gap between it and the gondolas, there was little risk of a collision. They made a clear, neat start, such a smart getaway that it attracted a certain amount of tourist attention, with children's arms waving and levelled cameras clicking.

"What price pictures now?" Gwen asked. She had turned her own head away when the cameras were raised, but Jake who was at the wheel had been steering the vessel, standing firm, balancing as he drove the launch through the wash of the vaporettos into the open waters beyond the mouth of the Grand Canal.

He gave her one furious look but could not spare thoughts or words to retaliate until he had driven the launch beyond the usual track of the smaller ferries and across the track of the big car-ferries and cargo boats in the main channel. Then he handed the wheel to the deck man and took Gwen below, pushing her on to one of the bunks before getting long cool drinks for them both.

"Now," he said. "What was that crap you shouted as we warmed up?"

"The tourists were taking pictures of us. Your man untying the boat."

"Casting off."

"You at the wheel and me, only I turned my head away."

"The glass would show just a reflection. Abe don't matter. Maybe they was all just tourists, too. I've hired the launch. Cash. All paid for. Two days."

Gwen listened but could not be bothered to take in the detail. All so familiar. Jake explaining his incredible cunning; his perfect arrangements; his masterly plans. So far successful this time with her help. But that had not

130

always been so. In America, by no means always successful. There had been the years when he was inside. Two stretches of three years. She had suffered the first time, had to work for her living. Not the last: there was more left in the kitty and available on demand.

Remembering other times of crisis and uncertainty as she looked across the cabin at Jake frowning into his glass, she wondered if this ostentatious launch, the show-off at the waterside, had to do with herself or with Owen or neither, some trouble he was keeping to himself.

"This guy," he said, filling his glass again but not offering to replenish hers. "He's here in Venice?"

"I told you he was in Florence, still following."

"Is he here?"

Thank God, she thought, that means Jake didn't see Owen slip away from behind Rose Lawler.

"Yes," she said. She dared not lie.

"You've seen him?"

"Over on the Lido, yes. Out of doors."

"What's he look like?"

She described a figure as unlike Owen as she could invent, with no distinguishing mark whatever.

"You're a big help. That all you can do?"

"Yes. I hardly know him." Jake's dissatisfaction was a measure of her success. But she must not overdo it.

However, Jake did not press her any further. She had done her duty, poor silly moll, in reporting Owen at all, which showed she understood the importance of the fact that this stranger had told her he saw her in Geneva. That was the crux of the matter. The guy must be bent, so was he a loner or did he belong to the opposition, to some hitherto unknown rival association, a competitor in the same line or even a political gang out for funds?

Gwen waited for more questions but none came. Nor did any other approaches or demands. This hurt her vanity but did not seriously disturb her. Her personal relationship with the old villain had become as conventional and restricted as a long-time marriage. That was why Owen had been such a welcome change. But she had better not let her thoughts wander to Owen. Jake was far too slick at reading her.

After another drink which this time she shared and a further ten minutes of brooding silence and inward speculation Jake moved to the companion way and going up three steps of it looked about him. Obedient to his orders his men had taken the launch past the western end of the Lido and were heading straight out into the Adriatic. In fact, as Jake found when he had reached the cockpit in rapid time, there was not much more than a blue-grey blur where he had expected to see a long yellow-strand.

With a few snarling oaths he took over the wheel, swung the boat half round, studied the chart beside him, waited for the compass to settle and then, more gradually, set a course to approach the land.

Gwen had been tossed on to the cabin deck by this unheralded movement. She scrambled up, vaguely alarmed and climbed into the wheelhouse herself. She had never liked the sea, had never got used to it, though Jake had taken her for many voyages short and long, over the years. Outside the protecting islands there was an only too distinct movement. Two stiff drinks on an empty stomach, five hours since lunch, gave little hope of escaping the worst.

"Where are we?" she said and added in an appealing voice, "Isn't it rather rough out here? I don't think ..."

"You can't be sick *now*," Jake told her roughly. "I need your help."

"Help? How?"

"Wait and see. And stay up here. You'll feel it less than below."

So she sat down in the cockpit, near the open door of the wheelhouse, looking wistfully at the Lido on the horizon, which presented a steady and steadily growing line in shape, size and colour, in contrast to the lazy, heaving waves that never stopped their hateful movement, up and down, side to side, slap and over, on and on . . .

It was Abe, who was acting as deck hand, who called, "Ain't we in close enough now, boss? This yere post ain't more'n couple hundred yards, I guess."

Jake lessened speed till the launch was almost still in the water, to Gwen's distress tossing far more uncomfortably than before. Abe went into the wheelhouse, Jake came out with a pair of long range binoculars hanging round his neck. He took them off and handed them to Gwen.

"Now," he said. "Focus on that bunch of bathers half-way between here and the sand. See any of your friends among them?"

Gwen had some trouble getting the glasses in focus, but at last she managed it.

"I don't think," she began. "Why, yes, I can see Mr. Banks."

"Who's he?"

"I told you. With the hippy daughter. Want to see?"

"No, no. Those schoolmarms. See any of them?"

"Oh!" So that was what he wanted. Her hints about Rose Lawler had registered. "No. They must have gone in. They did mean to come down to bathe. That's Mr. Banks in the shallow water near the shore. Heavy type. Not exactly fat."

He took the glasses and soon picked the figure she described. But he handed them back.

"Have another go," he said. "That feller couldn't rock your boat."

"The damn thing's rocking my stomach to bits right now," Gwen cried in desperation, trying once more, for Jake had altered them, to get the binoculars focused to her own vision. It was then she recognised Owen, lying on his back, gazing up at the sky.

Jake laughed suddenly, applauding her feeble sally while he encouraged her to try again. All this time the launch was moving again, straight in towards the shore. They must turn away soon or they would run Owen down. Jake was still gazing into the distance. Then Owen began to move. He must not see her, not with Jake again. Her sudden fright together with the movement of the launch were too much for her.

"I'm going to throw up," she gasped, pulling the binoculars from round her neck, pushing them into his hand. She stumbled and was sick on the deck of the cabin. After that she crawled on to a bunk, remaining there until the launch took her to the pier at the end of the bathing beach.

Jake paid no attention whatever to her distress. He was annoyed that she could not confirm any one of the figures he had picked out to be that of Mrs. Lawler. But having watched the various women bathers try to swim and then stand up and then try again, never drawing nearer to the limiting post than he was allowing the launch itself to approach, he came to the conclusion that his plan for the real retired schoolmarm had every chance of success. As he turned the launch away he had noticed one swimmer quite close by, making back towards the shore. But this was a man, a whitish body in trunks.

Meanwhile Abe had mopped up the vomit in the cabin, offered Gwen a glass of water, which she refused and was standing by for orders.

"Take the wheel while I watch the depth," Jake ordered. "Be ready to turn off when I say."

"Ya, boss," Abe said. They were, once more, moving in towards the shore.

Jake watched the echo-finder and the launch crept in again and once again turned off.

After that Jake took the wheel and cruised the launch up and down off-shore for twenty minutes. Then he took her back to his former position and moved very cautiously in-shore at various points, watching the echo-sounder carefully to see how far he could venture without stranding. By this time Owen was back on the beach, drying himself in the sun.

134

Gwen was below, still prostrate, the sea was empty now of bathers, so there was no one to tell Jake he had seen the man he had begun to fear, but by whom he was now himself feared. His men knew nothing whatever about Owen; neither had any orders except with regard to Rose Lawler, who had not appeared at this preliminary rehearsal.

At last Jake turned the launch away and drove her to the pier nearby where he tied up until Gwen was fit enough to make her own way back to the tour hotel. She protested and cried, as usual. She said he would be the death of her. She demanded a taxi. He gave her money to pay for one, but refused to leave the launch.

Owen left his room very early the next morning, found a continental breakfast at a nearby restaurant and returned a couple of hours later with an Italian newspaper. He sat in the hall lounge with the intention of waylaying Mr. Banks as he passed through on his way to or from the dining room.

He did not have to wait long and he saw, with some amusement that his intended victim was in no way surprised to see him. So he cut short his usual studied approach, folding his newspaper, rising at once and saying as he stepped forward, "Good morning, Mrs. Banks. Good morning, sir. May I have a few words with you?"

"We are going over to Venice," Mr. Banks said, continuing to walk towards the lifts.

"In the garden, perhaps," Owen said. Clearly the rush tactic was needed here.

"I cannot imagine . . ." Mr. Banks was beginning, when his wife interrupted.

"I'll go up and get our things," she said. "You talk to Mr. Strong. I'll come down to the garden when I'm ready. You won't want anything except your camera, will you?"

"I hope not," Mr. Banks said, with an ominous side glance at Owen.

135

The two men settled themselves on metal chairs in an open space, chosen by Mr. Banks. Some large trees near them provided a half-shade that grew deeper as the sun, continuing to rise in the sky, looked down through the thicker canopy of the trees' upper branches. This was to the advantage of both, since feelings ran higher as the interview developed.

Mr. Banks lost no time in making clear his general disapproval.

"I hope you found your wallet all right," he said, attacking from his position of the afternoon before.

"Yes, thank you," Owen answered steadily. He waited a few seconds and then added, "The wallet itself was under the bench in the changing room in the hut. The Italian notes were still there, but the travellers' cheques had vanished."

"Bad luck," said Mr. Banks. "I suppose you can get some more."

"Not immediately, I'm afraid. I was hoping perhaps you would — assist me."

Mr. Banks snorted. He had expected something very much less crude.

"You — *what*?" he said, with contempt as well as anger.

"I am leaving Italy today," Owen said, watching Mr. Banks closely. "I shall want fifty thousand lire."

"You're mad! You'll get nothing from me. I wouldn't lend you five lire, not a sou, a tanner, a two p. piece."

"I'm not asking you for a loan," Owen said, very gently. "I'm asking you for fifty thousand lire — in notes — cash."

Mr. Banks paled a little. Worse than the touch he'd expected. Blackmail. But he was not yet defeated.

"You bloody skunk!" he declared, striking the metal table between them so that it rang like a rusty alarm bell.

A waiter happened to be passing through the garden with a tray from one of the hotel annexe rooms. He heard what he took to be a call for his services and swerved to obey it.

"Two brandies," Owen said in Italian. The waiter shook his head.

"The bar is not open, signore," he said.

"Two coffees, then."

The man went away.

"I have ordered two coffees," Owen said. "I think he may forget the order."

"You can have them," Mr. Banks said, breathing hard. "I'm going."

He began to rise but Owen, slipping his right hand into his jacket pocket said, "No!" in such a hard voice that the other sank back into his chair.

"What makes you think..." he stammered, watching Owen's hand move in the pocket. "Why do you think I should dream of..."

"It is unfortunate," Owen said slowly, "that when you persuaded your daughter to join you on this charter tour you did not know the girl was pregnant."

"How dare you..."

"Please let me finish. She was smoking cannabis, too. You realised that. I suppose you and your wife had rows about her. Penelope got round you for money for her supplies, I imagine. But she couldn't get round the other business. She asked Mrs. Franks for advice. The fat midwife was sympathetic, but not helpful. I happen to know how Penny managed it and she started an abortion. But it was badly done. It became an emergency. She had to go to hospital."

Mr. Banks was staring at him in horror.

"You — you devil!" he panted. "You *couldn't* know!"

"But I'm right, aren't I? They treated her correctly in hospital. The doctors suspected at once, but the symptoms were confused. Hence that abortive typhoid scare. But they cleaned up the real abortion quite correctly as was their duty. Only they insisted the girl should go home and stay there."

Mr. Banks groaned.

"I do sympathise," Owen said. He had to push his chair back to avoid Mr. Banks's fist, but he went on speaking. "If she'd stayed away . . . But now . . . Well, it only needs my word about the name and misapplied activities of the so-called doctor in Rome . . . Abortion is not legal in this country, Mr. Banks . . . A longish term — Italian prisons . . . Very slow legal processes . . ."

Mr. Banks, white with rage and fear, got up from his chair.

"Stay where you are," he said. "You win, damn you. Leaving Venice, did you say?"

"Today."

"I'll get you the money now. If I see you here on the Lido again I'll go to the police. I don't believe there would really be any danger to Penny now."

"Only a public scandal. The newspapers, you know."

Again Mr. Banks made a threatening movement but thought better of it.

"I'll wait here until you bring me the lire," Owen promised. "After that you will not see me again in this hotel."

He sat on in the shade of the tree. He felt it was a little sad to have worked so hard with so much unpleasantness for so small an amount. But he could not risk asking for more. There must be no questions asked at the bank, no special arrangements to be made. It would be enough to get going and after Geneva . . . well . . .

Presently the waiter reappeared with a tray and two cups of coffee. Owen paid for them and continued to wait.

When Mrs. Banks appeared she seemed agitated to find him alone.

"Have some coffee," Owen said to her, smiling. "Reg suddenly found he had to go to the bank. But he'll be back soon."

138

Chapter XIV

THE NEXT DAY was the last the tour would spend in Venice. It had also been arranged for it to spend the afternoon on the highlight of the visit, a trip to the famous glassworks on one of the smaller islands.

Rose and her friends had put their names down to join this expedition. They no longer considered Gwen to be one of their group though she still came to their table for meals. It seemed clear to them now that she had met friends in Venice by previous appointment. She had never mentioned these friends, which was not surprising, Rose told the others, after describing the three daunting figures that had swept the girl away from St. Mark's Square on the morning after their arrival.

"With this afternoon booked we had better finish anything we want to do in Venice this morning," Myra said at the breakfast table. Gwen had not yet appeared; the others, as usual, were there at the opening of the dining room double doors.

"We can't. Finish, I mean," Flo said. "We've hardly seen any of the important pictures. I suppose we could get to a few of them."

"I must buy one or two small presents," Rose said. "I've been spending too much time taking photographs. And looking at buildings. I rather felt I'd had my whack

139

of pictures in Florence. Which shows I begin to wilt at a plethora of Renaissance art, I'm afraid."

"I don't see that you need feel guilty on that account," Myra answered her. "Let's just go around independently when we're ready and meet in the Square for coffee at eleven. Shopping and sight-seeing are quicker to manage solo, don't you think?"

The others agreed though they did travel across together. They separated as they left the vaporetto. Rose could not resist another visit to the cathedral to take a last look at the mosaics, the gleam of rich gold ornament, the calm, wise, untortured Christ. She promised herself, as she gazed at these splendours, to make a longer, quieter, visit to Venice at some future date. Then she went out into the turmoil of narrow streets, dark smelly water, pushing tourists and shop windows filled with a strange medley of rubbish and highly-skilled craftsmanship.

In the end she bought a few lace-decorated handker-chiefs. Not very exciting, but genuine, she explained to her friends.

"I think I'd have done better to look at pictures like you, Flo," she said, gazing rather enviously at the excellent reproductions Miss Jeans had gathered. "I could have given those instead of these things."

"But the lace is beautiful," Myra protested. "You certainly couldn't get anything like it at home."

"I expect you could in London if you knew where to go."

"At ten times the price."

"Well, perhaps," she put the handkerchiefs back in their wrapping and said defiantly, "I know one thing. I've seen all I want to of this famous glass. Hideous! Great ugly animals and birds in the crudest pink and blue! The old-fashioned Edwardian fingerbowls — my mother had some — were fussy, over-decorated, but not half as vulgar as these monstrosities. And they're *everywhere*!"

"For the tourists," Flo said sadly. "Not the Grand

140

Tour ones any more, just our wealthy plebs, bless their hearts."

She smiled at her friends, to excuse if only to herself, the vehemence with which she had spoken. For she refused to consider her attitude a snobbish one when it related to people earning, at what she felt were inferior jobs, anything up to twice as much as she did herself.

The discussion faded into lassitude as the three women sipped their coffee, ordered ices, listened to classical music and gazed at their neighbours, similarly occupied. It was only when Rose caught sight of Gwen Chilton with the three forbidding figures of the day before that she roused herself to point them out.

"On the right, in the sun, moving towards the boats, the most extraordinary set of toughs. D'you see where I mean? Only yesterday Gwen was looking terrified out of her life. Today she seems happy enough."

"I hope she doesn't bring them over here," Myra said. "I might get up and run. Anything more like *The French Connection* . . ."

"Or *The Godfather* . . ."

"You needn't worry. They'll be out of sight in a minute."

There was no further sign of Gwen's nasty-looking new friends when the three women, having finished their leisurely refreshment, wandered slowly to the waterside to go back to the Lido for lunch.

It was after this meal, at which Gwen did not appear, that Rose Lawler made up her mind she had seen quite as much as she cared to of Venetian glass.

"I know you love watching *processes*," she said to Myra. "I remember how you enjoyed that leather business in Florence. Well, so did I, actually. But then the end results were pretty and I adore the smell of real leather. But glass — no. I simply could not endure to see a huge blue swan emerging from a twirling lump of molten glass. Very highly skilled, no doubt. But not for me, I think."

"What will you do then?" Flo demanded.

141

"Oh, take a book into the garden here at first, I suppose. And then go for a swim."

"I expect you'll have to book again from here."

"Very likely."

Mrs. Lawler found this was not difficult. And when she reached the beach a couple of hours later she found she was told she would soon be alone.

So much the better, she decided. She left her watch with her money at the gate keeper's lodge. The woman attendant there remembered her from the day before and said, when she handed over the metal number on its rubber ring, "You go for a swim again, signora? A long swim, as yesterday?"

"That wasn't a long swim," Rose laughed. "But yes, I shall swim again."

"Be very careful, signora. Those warning posts are real, not for fun, you know."

"I'll be careful."

When she reached the hut Rose found the other occupants, not the Bankses this time, were packing up and about to leave.

"Going already?" she asked.

They laughed.

"We've been here since before two," the younger of the two women said. "Cooked quite enough by now."

The man, cooked a good deal more than enough, Rose thought, said impatiently, "Come on, girls. All set, surely?"

"He's overdone it," the older woman sighed. "And I nearly killed myself oiling his back."

"All three acres of it," added the other.

As it seemed that a quarrel, or at any rate a dreary argument was building, Rose smiled and went into the hut to change. She made a neat pile of her clothes, hesitated over the number ticket, then hid it in a pocket of her cotton slacks. The gate keeper would never give her property to anyone else; they had talked for several minutes

142

and the woman had already recognised her as someone who had been in the sea the day before.

After a brief warming in the afternoon sun Rose set off down the beach. There were a few bathers in the shallows but no one she recognised. Two men were attempting to swim a little farther out, but finding it frustrating. She stood up to watch them. They did not look like Italians, so she ventured to say, "Very shallow, even out here, isn't it?"

"Aye," one of them answered, in a north-country voice. "It is an all. No tide's not an advantage."

"It gets a bit better farther out," she said, letting herself drop forward again.

"Beyond t'post, it do," said the other man. "Sudden like. Thee need t'watch it."

"I will."

She pushed forward lazily, then stood again, watching the two men as they began their cheerful retreat. Then turning on her back she began a slow, beautifully executed back stroke, on and on in the peaceful mild ripple of this sheltered corner of a tideless sea, not a cloud overhead, the westerly sun still warm on her left cheek. This was heaven ... this was what ...

"Rose! Rose! It is you, Rose, isn't it?"

The voice came from behind her, from the sea. Gwen Chilton's voice. How the devil ...

Turning over, pushing herself up, treading water, for there was no bottom here, Rose found herself about ten yards from a fair-sized white launch that she recognised from the day before. Gwen was standing in the cockpit, waving to her, while two of her strange new friends stood, one on either side.

"Come aboard!" the black-haired, dark-faced one called.

"I don't think ..." she began, but the launch swept forward, cutting off her retreat, narrowing the distance between her and Gwen's reaching hand.

143

"You'll go aground," she protested, hoping to scare them off. This failed. There was nothing to do but reach for the rungs of a small ladder that had suddenly appeared just below where Gwen stood.

"I was just thinking of going back," she said. "I must, if I'm to be in time for a shower before dinner."

"You must have dinner with us," the dark man said. "Introduce us, Gwen, my dear."

"Mrs. Lawler, this is Jake," Gwen said.

"Then thank you Jake, I'm sorry, but I must be going."

Jake made a sign, the ladder rose a foot or two and as she let go her hold on the rungs strong hands seized her by the shoulders and lifted her inboard, dripping, breathless with shock, furious.

"I'm sorry, Mrs. Lawler, but you must be staying," said Jake.

The launch, its engines revving, propeller thrashing, reversed away, then made a tight turn, heeling so steeply that Rose would have shot overboard on the other side of the boat if Jake had not supported her.

"That would not do at all," he said. "The propeller can be very dangerous, you know. Terribly dangerous."

She knew then that her situation, her whole situation, was terribly dangerous. She understood with a sick feeling in her stomach that her knowledge of Gwen Chilton, liar, potential thief, was real, these associates of hers were real thugs, not film fantasies, and that their behaviour must be related to her knowledge. Gwen had told them she knew too much. Would they silence her by blackmail? Or did they mean to kill her?

She shivered, realising that her inward chill was combined with a physical state of coldness. She saw that Jake was looking at her, a cruel smile on his full lips.

"I'm cold," she said. "Have you got such a thing as a towel handy?"

"Sure," he answered, the smile widening to a hearty

144

appreciation of her manner. "Fetch the lady a towel, honey!"

"I'll come with you, Gwen."

Rose expected to be stopped but no move was made to do this, so she went below and with the ample towel Gwen provided she soon dried and warmed herself, stripping off the wet bathing dress and throwing it to Gwen who squeezed the water from it into the galley sink before hanging it up over the gas jets of the stove.

Jake's head and shoulders appeared at the head of the companion way. Mrs. Lawler managed a modest scream and pulled the towel more closely about her. But she was not the object of Jake's immediate concern.

"We'll have that meal in just an hour from now, Gwen love, and Mrs. Lawler will eat with us."

The dark face disappeared to Rose's relief. She would not have spoken in any case. The launch was at his command together with his two henchmen and his cowed mistress. Remembering Gwen's evident pleasure in Owen's company, Rose even felt a slight compassion for the poor stupid girl. Watching her as the bully barked his instructions from above deck, she understood very clearly that this now ageing young woman was no skilled criminal but a rootless, rudderless creature, who needed instruction by the day, the hour, the minute, even in an emergency. Dimly Mrs. Lawler began to see a way of using Gwen to aid her possible escape.

For escape she meant to attempt later that evening, if any way presented itself. So she sat still, huddled in her towel until Gwen brought her back her bathing dress, not fully dry but warm enough to put on.

"They'll be down here in a jiffy," Gwen said. "At least two of them will." She had turned on the cabin lights and shut the door at the top of the steps, standing against it as Rose discarded the towel. "My!" she said. "You don't look up to much, I will say."

145

"I hope your Jake will agree with you and stop frightening a poor old schoolmistress," Rose answered tartly. "Have you got a comb?"

All this time she had kept her bathing cap on, with the earflaps turned up, as much from habit as anything else. Now she pulled it off and shook out her short, greying locks.

Gwen supplied a small comb from her handbag and as she bent over Rose to give it to her she whispered, "It isn't my fault! I swear it!"

"When?" Rose whispered back. It was clear from Gwen's distracted manner that she might be near to death and if she was to have any chance of avoiding it she must know when the final approach would come.

But Gwen only shook her head and went back to the galley. Presently she came into the cabin again to lay the table for a meal for four.

Rose saw that it was now very nearly dark outside. She moved to the other side of the cabin. Yes, they were well out to sea, the shore lights were a long way off. But for a little while now she noticed less movement of the boat, less noise from the engines. Was that significant? Probably just a move to make the meal pleasanter, easier to serve. The last meal of her life, she wondered, still unnaturally calm.

Jake and his deck hand Abe came down into the cabin. Jake poured drinks, including a stiff dry martini for Rose. She drank it as a necessary prelude to what might be coming, but at the meal that followed, some savoury pasta, cold meat and salad, peaches and grapes, she ate very little and refused altogether the wine Jake offered her with mock deference.

"And now," she said boldly, when the others had all finished eating. "I really must go back to the Lido, Mr. — er — Jake."

He stared at her without expression.

"Yes," he said. And after a few seconds of silence, "Ya,

146

Mrs. Lawler, back to the Lido. O.K. O.K. Eh, Abe boy?"

"As yo' say, boss," Abe replied.

So the launch turned and made for the shore again, eating up the miles as the sky darkened and the lights ahead grew brighter. Rose stood beside Jake, tense, unbelieving and yet half inclined to trust that earlier feeling of unwilling hope. So she must play the part she had tried to sketch to Gwen, the silly old schoolmarm, given to curiosity and prying into the affairs of others. The final opportunity was nearly upon her.

When the end lights on the little pier were very nearly abeam she said, putting an anxious note into her voice, "It gets shallow very suddenly, Jake. Where the last of the posts sticks up. Only I don't see it yet."

"I know," he answered. He signalled to the third man who was driving the launch and Abe moved forward to the side of the cockpit. "You don't see that post yet because it's all of two mile in from here. Maybe you won't see it, not ever, Mrs. Lawler."

"What d'you mean?" She knew well enough but there was only one chance for her, to get back in the sea alive and whole. "I expect I can swim in from where you picked me up."

"But I say you'll have to swim in from here, ma'am."

"But I couldn't. *I couldn't*! *I'd drown*!"

"Found drowned," Jake told her, savouring the words with open pleasure, rolling them off his tongue, repeating them with full, deep-throated American intonation that made them doubly horrific.

"Why? What have I done? How have I ever . . . ?"

"Because you bin tormenting my little Gwen," he said. "You bin interfering with my orders to her, my instructions. So I rub you out, see, an you don't interfere no more, never."

"You can't do it!" Rose cried wildly, so terrified by the big brute's manner and looks that she nearly dived overboard while he was still speaking. In fact she took a step away from him and saw the glint of a knife in Abe's hand that checked her.

"You can't mean me to *drown*," she forced out, recovering.

"I do mean just that," Jake answered. He was enjoying the situation. He had got that squeak of fear from her at last, the buttoned-up British bitch. He played for another.

"I can't use the gun," he said. "Nor yet the knife. I can't clobber that lousy superior dial. I want it natural — just natural goddam egg-head fool action. *So!*" he yelled and Abe at this signal sprang at Rose, lifted her sheer off her feet and threw her into the sea.

She let herself meet it with the stinging splash of a full belly-flop. It nearly winded her, but she let herself sink, then bobbed up again, on her back now, to let out a water-clogged scream, followed by a cry for help.

The two figures at the side of the cockpit had been joined by a third. Gwen, that must be Gwen.

"Gwen!" she shouted. "They've murdered me, Gwen!"

The launch's engines that had been idling, revved into loud noise, the vessel began to move. Rose continued with her feeble attempts to swim away. She remembered she had shown she could manage a few yards out of her depth when the thugs hi-jacked her. She must not do less than that now. Besides they would hang about until Jake decided she was dead.

Indeed they did. They had a searchlight, too. They came swinging back, looking for her, so she sank herself, except for her head, arms and shoulders and as the light reached her, flung up her hands, gave a choking cry and sank below the surface.

"That's fixed her," Jake said with satisfaction.

"That's fixed her good and proper, boss," Abe agreed as the searchlight was switched off, the launch turned and began to move towards the lighted pier where Gwen had disembarked the day before.

Mrs. Lawler had been too far away to hear these conclusions, but in any case she would not have done so, for she was swimming under water as fast as she could until her breath gave out and she had to surface. It was not a record underwater swim, but not a bad one either, she decided. At any rate the launch was some distance off, showing only its port navigation light, the green one. That meant it would land Gwen at the pier, probably. So the girl would reach the hotel first, she told herself and settled down to the long swim before her.

A couple of miles, she thought, which should be well within her powers, provided she took it quietly, provided her breathing settled, provided her ageing heart, already disturbed by the terrors of the evening, did not let her down. Provided her calculation of the distance, difficult to measure at sea level, at night, a moonless night, thank God, or those murderous devils would have seen her surface...

She swam on, keeping her course fixed by the pattern of the shore lights, until with thankfulness and relief the pattern was interrupted by a dark object that appeared among them, gradually increasing in height and width and presently beginning to move away to the left.

The post! The tall upright post marking the limit for non-swimmers. At last! At last!

In her joy she put on a little spurt, then, terrified by the mess she made of it, turned on her back to rest, before again starting to move soberly towards the shore. It was a token of her growing weakness and her knowledge of it that she was well inside the safety limit before she dared to test the depth of the water.

As she stood up at last with the sea breast high only, she staggered, everything swam about her. Another sign of age. She had experienced this before in earlier times after a really long swim, say for two hours or more. A matter of balance; the middle ear. Only now, after perhaps a mere half hour...

Her progress to the beach, first mostly swimming, then

149

plodding wearily, took almost as long, she was ready to believe, as the perilous swim before it. When she finally left the water and crept rather than walked up the long slope to the huts, she found the darkness increased, since the tall road lights were now hidden by the boundary hedge. She could only peer at the doors of the huts as she reached them, feel for the handles and push. Not that it made any difference, for her towel, her clothes, were still denied her. Every hut was locked, the chairs and tables all cleared away.

Rose sat down on the sand and burst into loud, indignant, childish sobs.

Chapter XV

THE NIGHT WATCHMAN heard the sobbing. He was at the time making his second tour of the huts, walking along between the front row that lined the beach itself and the second row behind it. His first thought was that the sound came from a trespassing child, lost in the dark, unable to find again the hole through which he had crawled in. Very unlikely that. He knew them, the cunning little devils. Then could it be some outraged girl, deserted by her seducer, or even an abandoned tart, cheated of her earnings?

He traced the sounds to their source to find he was wrong in all his guesses. It was none other than the mad Englishwoman, who stopped her abandoned grief at the sound of his approaching footsteps and was scrambling to her feet as he appeared.

The gate keeper had told him about the mad English-woman when he came on duty before she left.

"She is very tall and thin," the gate keeper said. "Also quite old, but extremely active. She is fond of swimming and indeed swims very well. But reckless, like so many of her race. And self-willed. Married, but a widow. No control for many years, one would suppose. She has not yet come up from the beach."

"So what?" he had asked.

"So you work as usual. You lock the huts as usual."

"And if I find this Englishwoman's clothes and her towel?"

"She is sure to be in by dark. But if not, you bring her things here and lock that hut as well."

"And notify the police?"

The gate keper had considered.

"Not immediately. She may be mad, but not stupid, I feel sure. But she could over-estimate her strength, perhaps."

"Being old, as you say."

"Being less strong than she feels she is. After midnight, if she has not come in, you may notify her hotel. Let them notify the police."

The night watchman thought this was the right way to go about things. At nightfall he collected Mrs. Lawler's clothes, securing at the same time the metal tag with the number of her locker at the gate house. At half-past eleven he set out on his second round of the huts. It was then that he discovered Mrs. Lawler, guided by her sounds of distress.

When she saw the dark figure of a man behind the torch he directed at her, Rose was uncertain whether to scream or run away. But the voice she heard was reassuring.

"Do not be alarmed, signora," the voice, an elderly one, told her in slowly spoken Italian. "I see you have been bathing. Am I right in believing you are an English signora, with a tourist party from England?"

Rose did not understand the whole of these remarks, but she did realise that the man was some sort of official and that he thought he knew who she was or at any rate knew her nationality.

"You are right," she answered in Italian and continued partly in that language but chiefly in English to tell him she had been for a long swim and was upset when she found the hut locked and so could not change back into her clothes.

"I have them safe at the lodge," the night watchman

told her, pointing his torch in the direction of the gate house. "Come with me."

He shone the torch on the ground and walked beside the dripping mad woman, who stumbled a little when they left the soft sand for the gravel paths above the beach, but otherwise gave no trouble. He took her inside where her clothes and towel lay on a chair. Her metal number was in his own pocket.

"Have you the number of your locker?" he asked.

Mrs. Lawler did not understand. He took out the disc, holding it upside down.

"My number?" She thought hard. "Yes, I left it with my clothes."

She gave him the number she remembered. He turned the disc over. It corresponded. For the first time the night watchman smiled. This was indeed the right mad English-woman. She had not drowned. The gate keeper was right. But so tall, so thin, so lacking in all a woman should be.

"I must change," Mrs. Lawler said, stooping forward to pick up her towel and beginning to dry herself.

"I wait outside," the night watchman said hastily, stepping to the door. Mrs. Lawler laughed.

There was no difficulty about securing the rest of her possessions. The night watchman had access to Rose's small locker where she found her watch, her handbag with her wallet, passport, make-up things and handkerchief inside, together with a cardigan she had provided in case the late afternoon grew cold.

This last she greeted with a little cry of joy that made the night watchman knock at the door to ask if she had need of help. She told him to enter, which he did with mis-givings, wondering what he would see. But it was simply the mad lady fully dressed, even to the ubiquitous woollen garment now worn world-wide by women on the upper halves of their bodies. On Mrs. Lawler, together with her equally regrettable but usual trousers, they took away all trace of the fantastic, the disturbing, effect of an elderly female, just out of the sea, prostrate on the sand, crying her heart out.

Besides, his problem was now solved. The last of the bathers was disposed of. Very often it had been a couple, enjoying a moonlight bathe or a love-making, full of apology for their late departure and a tip for his tolerance. He had never yet found occasion to notify the police or the hotels, for was it not the holiday season, a time for indulgence?

The night watchman escorted Mrs. Lawler to the gate, which he unlocked for her with a flourish. She presented him with a generous tip and an expression, in her halting Italian, of thanks for his kindness. He watched her walk away with a steady gait, not fast but perfectly firm.

It was not until the next evening, when he described the whole occurrence to the gate keeper, that he heard its possible explanation.

"I was warning a party not to stay on too long or swim out too far," she said. "when a gentleman told me 'We saw an odd thing yesterday. A woman tourist was picked up by a launch just outside the bathing limit. It went out to sea with her and never came back as long as we were down on the beach.' That could have been your lady."

"I suppose so. But why not land her at the pier?"

"In her swimming costume?"

"But so late. Nearly midnight. I was about to ring up her hotel when I found her."

They both shrugged. It was inexplicable.

Rose got back to the hotel at half-past twelve. The front door was open, there was one young man at Reception, reading a newspaper by the light of one lamp on the desk. He handed her the key of her room without comment, returning immediately to his paper.

"Thank you," Rose said. "Can you tell me if Mrs. Chilton has come in?"

154

The young man lifted his eyes, polite but totally uninterested.

"You know the number of her room?"

Rose gave it. She felt foolish. There were very few gaps in the rows of keys. At this hour of the night — morning, now, of course — gaps due to absent guests were probably very few. Night life on the Lido could not be so very extensive. Or not for 'Roseanna's' tourist patrons, anyhow.

So Gwen was back. Rose took the lift to her own room first. She was by now desperately tired. Her arms and legs ached with growing stiffness; her head ached from exhaustion and an unaccustomed twelve-hour fast. But she could not rest. Those wicked men and their weak, silly accomplice had meant to kill her and had failed. She must escape at once, from any further possible contact with them. Myra and Flo would be in bed and asleep two hours or more. In any case, much as she liked their company, they were not real friends. She shrank from confiding in them the wider implications of her present predicament.

For it was true she had tried to find out more about Gwen Chilton than she had ever imagined she would try or even want to do. And she knew she had done this simply on Owen Strong's account, because she pitied him for his wartime injuries, because Charles had suffered in like manner, because of the lasting guilt for Charles's death she could not surmount even now, twenty-seven years later.

So what should she do? Go to bed, get up in a few hours' time, appear at breakfast with a joking story of late bathing, watch Gwen's shock at her reappearance, see the girl go quickly to the telephone and then what? Wait for Jake to strike again, in Verona, in Cremona, their final one night stop, even at Genoa Airport. Even on the plane going home!

But Gwen was weak, obedient to her evil master, but not always totally complaisant. So the best plan, the only plan, was to intimidate Gwen. Frighten her off telling Jake

155

his intended victim had tricked him. Jake would blame her for knowing so little about Mrs. Lawler after travelling with her for nearly two weeks. She would impress this upon Gwen. And keep her away from a telephone for the rest of the trip? It couldn't be done, she told herself.

But still she could not rest. To be in bed would only mean to lie awake while the aches and pains grew. Impossible. Pulling on the white summer coat in which she had left England but never worn since then, she went along to Gwen's room which was on the same floor and knocked at the door.

She had to knock three times before she heard a reluctant hand unloosing a bolt and then turning a lock. The door opened, Gwen fell back with a low cry, instantly suppressed, and Rose stepped forward. Owen, holding the collapsing girl with a hand over her mouth, pushed her into Mrs. Lawler's arms while he re-locked the door, bolted it and put the key in his own pocket.

They were both very scantily clothed, Rose noted, if clothed at all but only wrapped, one in a flimsy dressing gown and the other in a towelling beach coat. She pushed Gwen into a chair, turned and said briskly. "*You* here! Well, I *am* glad!" So she was, for she saw a possible real escape from her fear and danger.

"Yes, it's me," he answered. "And may I express an equal pleasure in seeing you. Gwen has just led me to suppose . . ."

"Gwen is a very silly girl," Mrs. Lawler said, as severely as she could. "She exaggerates."

"She's a compulsive liar," Owen said. "But I think this time she was trying to tell me the truth."

"You two . . ." Gwen struggled to speak. "Bloody liars yourselves! She said she couldn't swim, not far, she said. She acted like . . . like . . ."

Gwen began to cry. Neither of the others took any further notice of her.

"Seriously," Rose said. "There was an attempt on my

156

life. It failed because they were so intent on faking a natural bathing accident."

She went on to tell him what had happened from the moment she was kidnapped and forced on board the launch. She explained how she had recovered her clothes and valuables. The old watchman had taken no steps about her absence. She was asked no questions at the reception desk when she reached the hotel. She saw from the key board that Gwen had got back before her.

"So you came along to take the mickey . . ."

"Far more than that. Owen, they mean to kill me. If they know they've failed, they'll try again. I don't know why, but I'm sure of it."

"Gwen knows why. Tell her, darling."

Gwen had stopped crying when she saw no one was interested. She sat up straight and said sulkily, "I've got to finish the bleeding tour, then Jake will pick me up at Gatwick and we'll go to Geneva to pick up the bag from my safe deposit. Now the heat's off."

"You understand?" Owen asked politely.

"I understand she's more than just the little hotel thief I took her for," Mrs. Lawler answered.

"How dare you . . ."

"Belt up!" Owen told her savagely and once more the tears flowed, disregarded. He went on, "I agree you are in danger, Mrs. Lawler, Rose, if I may. Gwen, too, is now in danger. Since these thugs have never seen me, I am not in danger. Nor can they trace me."

"I had to tell Jake you'd booked into this hotel," Gwen interrupted.

"I am due to leave it in a few hours' time," he went on, making no answer to this. "I have a hired car in the ferry car park. I intended to drive to Geneva in any case. Now I propose to take you both with me. Gwen has already agreed to come with me, haven't you, love?"

She did not answer, but nodded, wiping her eyes.

"So if you care to come with us, Rose, you can get a

157

plane from Geneva back to England. Jake's lot could never sort all that out. Once safely there you can set the dicks on him if you want to. Interpol would help them to pick him up, but I think he'd be back in the U.S. by then."

"And Gwen?"

"Well, we'll probably make a go of it, won't we, honey?"

Again Gwen was silent. Poor Owen, Mrs. Lawler thought, these compassionate efforts seldom come off. The girl's no good, basically corrupt, unreformable. In her continued indulgence towards Owen, Rose was ready to ignore his obviously criminal intention to secure whatever it was Gwen held at Geneva, not to mention his already established relationship with her, a breach of the moral code Mrs. Lawler had been reared in. How could she blame him, when he had just shown her the way to safety?

"Tell me how all this can be done?" she said.

Owen explained. He repeated that he had a car at the ferry car park on the Lido. He would bring it to the hotel, or better perhaps send it with a chauffeur to pick up both the women and their suitcases in time to catch the first ferry out that morning. He was not sure of the time but it would be about four or half-past. He himself would take over from the chauffeur at the ferry.

"I must let Billie, our courier, know we are going," Rose said. "I should like to leave a note for one of my friends, too."

Owen thought, then said, "Why not put a note for the courier into your letter to the friend and leave the letter at Reception for her to get when she goes down at the usual breakfast time. We don't want anyone to know earlier than that."

He jerked his head towards Gwen as he spoke.

"Gwen and I will stay together all the time, won't we, Gwen?" Rose said. "No second thoughts yet again. Promise."

"I promise. After what Jake did ... Tried to do ..."

"Forget all that, love," Owen told her. "You follow Rose from now on." He made for the door, Rose at his heels.

"Are you actually *staying* in this hotel?" she asked, as he unfastened the door, this time leaving the key in the lock. He surely could not have come in and gone to Gwen's room clad only in a beach robe?

"Two nights paid in advance," he answered with a wide grin. "But not under the name you know me by."

It was a curious way of putting it; a warning really, though she failed to understand this.

He added, in a whisper, "Stick with her. Don't at any price, let her use the phone."

"I won't," she answered, but could add nothing for he was already gone, with the speed and silence she had observed in Rome, in Florence.

She turned back into the room, this time the one to secure the key. Gwen had not moved.

"Well, you heard the plan," she said, trying to keep the desperate weariness from her voice. "Pack your things, Gwen, then you can bring your case to my room and watch me while I do my own packing. We must get a move on if we're to be ready in time."

Chapter XVI

THEY WERE READY in very good time. While Gwen packed her bag Rose wrote a brief note to Myra to explain that she had found it necessary to leave the 'Roseanna' tour in Venice, but hoped she would see something of her and of Flo when they were all back in England. She gave her home address. She asked Myra to give the enclosed note to Billie.

To the courier she wrote that owing to unforeseen circumstances she and Mrs. Chilton were obliged to leave Venice in advance of the tour and return to England. She apologised for giving no notice of their intention. She would write to the travel firm and the travel agency who had arranged her personal trip. Her action had nothing whatever to do with the tour, which she had enjoyed very much and regretted leaving.

As she wrote these notes she kept Gwen in sight but the latter made no attempt either to attack her or to get at the telephone, which was at Mrs. Lawler's elbow on the table. When Gwen had finished they moved to Rose's room and the action was reversed.

But Gwen had no letter to write and Rose was now moving to and fro filling her two suitcases, one large, one smaller. Again Gwen remained quiet. She even offered to carry Mrs. Lawler's larger case as well as her own single one. The lift was working, however, and the distance to it was short. Rose kept control of her own baggage.

The same night clerk was at Reception when they gave up their keys and settled their outstanding petty accounts, such things as the use of the beach hut, for which Rose paid with a sense of irony. After that they sat down at a little distance from the desk and waited.

The car was punctual. The chauffeur walked in, small, dark, Italian, wearing a creased suit and a chauffeur's cap, which he took off when he saw the ladies.

"For the ferry, signora?" he asked, looking at Mrs. Lawler.

"You come from Signor Strong?" she asked.

"Si, signora," he answered, with a little smile she did not understand.

He took up all the bags and walked out of the hotel. The clerk at Reception eased himself into the doze that had been interrupted by the mad Englishwoman and her friend.

At the ferry park Owen took over. He paid Tito for his services and dismissed him. As soon as it was allowed he drove on to the waiting vessel. He would be one of the last to get off, but he preferred to have the shelter of the ferry's deck as early as possible. The vessel filled up with lorries and three other private cars. No coaches. They left punctually on time.

There were already lights in the upper enclosed deck. Mrs. Lawler remembered the coach's voyage over to the Lido. There had been coffee and small things to eat up there. Perhaps now.

"I'm literally starving," she said to Owen. "I want to go and see if the ferry restaurant is open."

"You do that," he said. "I'll stop with Gwen in the car. That is if we don't both come up too, now we've got going."

"I don't want anything," Gwen said sulkily. "Only to leave this bloody place."

161

"You're an effing bore," Owen told her, with careful moderation of his language.

There was coffee, French breakfast coffee at that. Also biscuits and with the advent of a body of workmen from the deck below, some hot dogs, copying the American basic dish. Rose ate two of these and drank two large coffees and bought two packets of biscuits, praising heaven for the spread of international foods in foreign lands. Then she went down to the car.

The dawn was breaking and the ferry terminal only a few minutes away.

"I nearly sent Gwen up to find you," Owen said reproachfully.

"Sorry. But I couldn't have gone on otherwise. I'll be all right now for another twelve hours if necessary."

"You had dinner on the launch," Gwen broke in suddenly.

"You did. I daren't eat. Never did before a long swim."

"As a matter of interest," Owen asked. "What would you call a really long swim?"

"The Channel at Dover-Gris Nez is about twenty-six miles. But the tides setting across it make it longer."

Owen laughed, stopped to say, "Poor old Jake!" and laughed again. "You didn't brief him right, love, did you?" he said at last, giving Gwen a firm hug as the ferry bumped to rest at the terminal.

In twenty minutes they were clear of Venice and driving across the causeway. In half an hour they were on the autostrada route to Milan.

Mrs. Lawler had insisted upon sitting in the back of the car, leaving Gwen to Owen's supervision from now on. She knew she could stay awake no longer. In fact as the car settled into a steady seventy miles an hour on the great dual-carriageway road she curled herself up on the wide seat and was instantly asleep.

She did not wake up until Owen stopped the car in Verona. Time for breakfast, he announced, shaking her

162

shoulder gently. She responded at once, still tired but alert enough to take charge of Gwen while Owen found a parking place.

From Verona, much refreshed, they travelled on along the Po valley, past Brescia, past Bergamo until, north of Milan, they turned towards the western group of the great lakes and stopped for the third time that day at Lugano, where the dual carriageway came to an end and the mountains rose before them, tier upon tier into the far distance.

They had crossed the frontier without trouble of any kind, Rose reflected, as she stretched her legs and drew in deep breaths of the already cooler air. She looked about her. Owen had gone into the small hotel to order lunch. Gwen . . . well, where was Gwen? With Owen? She had not seen her move, so enthralled had she been by this first real view of Switzerland. For she had not left the car when they stopped at the frontier as they crossed from Italy, so anxious had she been that Gwen's papers and perhaps Owen's, might not be in order.

With no excuse for lingering she hurried into the hotel. Owen was at the reception desk, Gwen approaching him from a door labelled to show it was a double cloakroom. "Dames", "Messieurs". Rose felt safer already. French was a long familiar tongue. Italian fascinating, but far more alien.

"Where do we go from here?" she asked Owen, as they settled to their meal.

"Geneva," he answered, briefly.

"Yes. But how?"

"Wait and see."

Gwen looked up at him with something like scorn. Since the meal began she had seemed to recover from her persistent withdrawal. This surprised Mrs. Lawler and also Owen, who had found a totally silent unresponsive companion in the front seat a growing bore.

"We have to go across the Gotthard Pass, of course," Gwen stated firmly. "Or through it on a train."

163

The others were surprised.

"Have you done this before?" Mrs. Lawler asked.

"Who told you?" Owen said sharply.

Gwen lowered her eyes and returned to her food. Mrs. Lawler watched Owen consult a rather tattered map he took from his pocket. After the meal she searched the hall of the little hotel and found, as she hoped, a small stand with an up to date AA continental handbook for sale. It was bent at the edges and very dusty. Probably tourists had consulted it without paying for the privilege. Ashamed of all English-speaking frauds she bought the book and took it back to the others.

"The through railway is marked," she said when she had established this.

"So it is," Owen agreed. "With room in the back for cars, too."

"You knew that?"

"Oh yes, I knew." He glanced at Gwen who was sipping her coffee and did not appear to be interested. But he saw the saucer shake in her hand and the coffee spill. She jumped up and made for the door.

"After her!" Owen ordered.

Mrs. Lawler found Gwen beginning to put through a telephone call to a number in Bergamo. She was able to stop the call going through. Gwen took it quietly.

"Who were you trying to get in Bergamo?" Owen demanded as they rejoined him.

"Billie," she answered without hesitation.

"Nonsense," Rose told her. "They were having lunch in Verona and going on to Cremona for tonight."

"Nowhere near Bergamo," Owen added. He looked at his watch and jumped up.

"On we go, girls," he said cheerfully, making for the waiting car.

This time he put Mrs. Lawler in the front, to see the view, he told her, and Gwen in the back, to watch the road behind.

"Why?" she asked, sulkily.

"Don't you know?"

Her answering flush told him his guess was probably right and that he had better keep a more than usually careful eye on his rear window.

"You can navigate too, if you will, Rose," he said as he got into the driver's seat. "Your map's a bit small scale but it's more recent than mine. We start up the valley then climb leftish to the Gotthard at Airolo, where we find the train . . . God willing . . ." he added, under his breath.

The valley was in shadow, but shafts of sun began to slant across the road as they climbed. At Airolo they joined a line of cars waiting to go through the railway tunnel, avoiding the open pass. Owen stopped the engine and got out, to stand looking back down the road, his hand on the rear door handle. Mrs. Lawler did the same on the other side. She knew or guessed what Owen feared. Gwen knew too, but she sat stiffly on the back seat, staring forward, silent as ever.

They had to wait nearly an hour before the queue moved. It was now just after one in the afternoon. To Mrs. Lawler, for whom yesterday had passed and merged into the present, the continued brightness of the day was astonishing. True they had breakfasted at seven, and lunched at half-past eleven. But now to find it only just after one . . .

The cars moved slowly on to the train, Owen and Mrs. Lawler got back into their seats. The space in front filled, grew less, Owen moved on, bumper to bumper, careful, persistent.

There was an argument in front. He moved on very gently. No room! Yes, just room! Yes, there *must* be room!

For Gwen sat forward suddenly, fumbling for the door handle and Mrs. Lawler swung round in her seat, leaned over to beat Gwen's hand from the handle.

165

"Look behind, Owen!" she gasped, still fighting off Gwen.

He had already looked. A big black car, more powerful than the one Tito had found for him, was coming up the road fast. He did not need to see the faces: the heads and headgear told him who they were.

Owen had not stopped moving and was now driving very slowly up the ramp into the train, though the argument in mixed Italian and French had not stopped. But his calm insistence, together with the fact that there really was room for one but only one more car, triumphed in time. As he put on the brake and switched off the engine, he turned to look at Gwen.

"You bloody goddamed bitch!" he said with such cold steel in his voice that even Rose's besotted confidence was shaken.

"When . . .?" Rose began.

Gwen turned to her with a vicious look.

"Never you mind, you silly old cow!" she snapped. "Needn't think you could keep your eye on me every bloody minute. He'd kill me if I didn't report as he ordered."

"Judging by his expression as we beat him to the train he'll do that anyway," Owen said. Gwen inevitably began to cry.

The tunnel seemed to Mrs. Lawler to go on for ever. But at last they came again into daylight and at the first station, Andermatt, they left the railway. This was done easily and quickly, since Owen's car had been the last to go on and therefore was the first to drive off. He wasted no time as he did so and very soon they were driving up the straight approach to the Furka Pass.

Mrs. Lawler was still in the front seat of the car. If she had not been so terrified of nemesis behind them, she would have been delighted with their magnificent surroundings, the great mountain glacier on their right, the wide view rising to further heights on the left.

166

But as they came to the beginning of the twists and turns, the sharp bends and unexpected loops in the road, she clung to the strap of the door handle, thankful for her safety belt, thankful she was on the right hand side of the continental car, thankful she was not in Owen's place, the side of the drop. Not that they sped along the edge of a precipice; the land fell away very steeply from the road, covered closely with pines; but it fell for thousands of feet and she could imagine the car plunging and somersaulting and crashing through the trees as it fell. Owen must have realised the danger, too, for he slowed up after one rather dangerous skid on a bend, slowed up and then swung into a space on the right below overhanging rocks and stopped.

"Listen!" he said gently.

They all heard it, a car on the road behind them. Just forty minutes since they left Andermatt, Mrs. Lawler saw, taking a swift look at her watch.

"Stay where you are, both of you!" Owen ordered.

He was out of the car, running back, disappearing round the buttress of rock that hid them from the road behind.

Gwen flung herself at the rear door of the car, wrenched it open and was out, also running back, disappearing behind the rock as Owen had done a few seconds before.

Rose had some difficulty in following. Owen had parked so near the wall of rock that she could not get out of the door beside her but had to slide across the driver's seat. She did not attempt to run, she was still too stiff from her long swim and the hours of driving. But she moved fast enough for all that, trying to catch up with Gwen. She saw the girl, still running, disappear round the next corner of the road.

The sound of the oncoming car was louder now, nearer. Mrs. Lawler broke into a desperate sort of sprint, shouting "Gwen! Gwen, come back!"

She could not remember afterwards in quite what order everything happened from that moment. There was a shot

167

and a scream. She rounded the bend of the road and she found Owen at her side. Gwen was lying on her face where she had been stopped by the shot. Jake's car, not fifty yards away was still advancing. Abe, with a long handled gun was leaning from the front passenger seat, taking aim.

"Get down!" Owen yelled, dropping to one knee.

As she did so she saw that he held a pistol and was pointing it at the advancing car. But she dropped to her own knees beside Gwen, instinctively putting up both arms as she did so, which made her lose her balance so that she toppled over beside the prostrate girl.

She heard another scream, two more shots, Jake's car roaring close. The end, she thought, shutting her eyes, thinking of her son, whom she would never see again, his wife whom she would never meet.

Then her frozen senses were aware of a different noise. Shouts, hoarse screams, the crashing of trees, splintering, falling metal clanging, thumping. The whole receding, but repeated until at last, at long last, silence, blessed, blessed silence.

Am I dead, she wondered, still not daring to move. And Owen, and Gwen? Are we all dead, at peace at last?

Chapter XVII

"ARE YOU ALL right?"

It was Owen's voice and Owen's hands gently turning her over. She gasped, looked up at him, tried to smile.

"I think so." With an effort she remembered. "Of course I'm all right. It was Gwen ... Gwen! They shot her ..."

She sat up, then got to her knees again. Gwen had vanished.

"No," Owen said. "I've taken her to the car. She's hurt, but not badly. But I need your help. Can you get up?"

Rose got to her feet with his strong hands lifting her. She looked back down the road. A rifle lay there.

She remembered more. The man Abe, pointing it at her, throwing it away as he screamed. Herself dropping to the ground, over-balancing.

"He could have killed me," she said slowly. "But he thought I was a ghost, drowning again as he thought he saw me drown last night, my arms thrown up as I sank." She stared at Owen. He had heard her describe her escape from the launch, but had he understood?

"So that was it," he breathed. "Providential, Rose, for all of us."

"Gwen," she said, beginning to walk away. No need to ask about Jake, the car, or any of those three abominable ruffians. She remembered all those noises and interpreted them without difficulty. If Owen's pistol had any part in

169

their final fatal swerve from the road, he was not to be blamed. If any of them lived, it was not her responsibility, nor his to find out. But Gwen, that was different.

She found that Owen had pulled a rug from the car and laid the girl on it, with his own rolled-up jacket under her head. His handkerchief was tied round her shoulder, but it was already soaked through with blood.

There had been a pool of blood where she had lain on the road.

"My suitcase," Mrs. Lawler ordered. "Quick, Owen!"

He brought it to her. She dived into the car for her handbag to get her keys. Gwen's bag was on the back seat where she had left it.

"Open it," she ordered, throwing the keys to Owen. "Get out a long white cotton petticoat and tear it into strips about nine inches wide. My hands are too dirty."

She wiped the road dust off on the rug before she began, very gently, to take away the blood-soaked handkerchief. The wound, when it was exposed, was messy but neither very wide nor deep. It was, however, awkwardly placed, being just below the collarbone, between it and the shoulder joint itself.

Owen worked quickly and was soon handing long cotton strips to Rose. She folded one into a pad to push against the ragged wound itself. With Owen holding the arm close, she bound the next across the wound and shoulder joint, with a twist round the upper arm to give leverage. She repeated this with a third strip, taking the end over the opposite shoulder.

"Now a sling," Mrs. Lawler said. "You'll find three scarves down the left hand side of the case. Give me the green and brown one, it's the longest."

While he was searching Gwen opened her eyes.

"Don't talk," Mrs. Lawler said. "Those devils shot you, but not badly. This is First Aid. We'll soon have you in hospital with proper treatment."

"Not hospital," Gwen said faintly.

"Don't talk."

They lifted her on to the back seat of the car and Rose got in beside her to take the stricken girl's head on her lap and protect her injured left shoulder from jolts and swerves.

Of these there were many as they drove cautiously over the pass and began the long descent. But Owen seemed to know his way. He asked no questions nor looked at the map. Rose forced herself to stay awake. The excitements of the last few hours, together with the removal of Jake and his friends had brought her once again to the edge of exhaustion. Gwen, suffering now from severe shock, sank into a semi-conscious state, broken from time to time by sudden twinges of pain. Soon they would be down from the mountain, Rose thought, some town nearer than Geneva, where Gwen could find a hospital bed and the necessary surgery for her wound.

When the great lake came into view for the first time through the tree belt that surrounded them Rose put this to Owen. But he shook his head.

"No go," he said. "We've got to make Geneva. Got to get her case from the bank before it closes."

Mrs. Lawler was outraged.

"She can't!" she cried. "She can't possibly do such a thing! There isn't time, anyway!"

"There will be time — just about. You said yourself the wound wasn't deep."

"I'm not a doctor!" Mrs. Lawler was still indignant. "I said it didn't *look* deep, or dangerous. But the bullet . . ."

"Never mind the bullet," he said rudely and called out to Gwen, "How does it feel now, love?"

"I'm thirsty," Gwen answered, rallying. "My mouth's as dry as — as dust."

"Will you be all right if I prop you up while I get at the thermoses?" Mrs. Lawler asked anxiously.

"Have to be," the girl muttered, but she did nothing to help herself and it was quite a struggle for Mrs. Lawler to lift her away into a sitting position. Gwen moaned but did not scream, she coughed and retched but did not vomit. And when Rose gave her some ice-cold mineral water she sipped it eagerly and seemed to feel better afterwards.

Looking at her watch for the first time since the battle on the mountain top, as she described it to herself, Mrs. Lawler saw to her astonishment that the time was no more than three-thirty. The whole episode from leaving Andermatt and the railway had taken little more than an hour. The actual encounter must have been over in a matter of minutes. Well, that was reasonable. Such violence, with those particular results, could not have been other than brief.

As Owen had promised they reached Geneva about ten minutes before the banks were due to close. Gwen gave the name of the one where she had deposited her case, but of course Owen knew it already.

"I know it," he agreed.

He drew up at the steps and got out to help Gwen. Mrs. Lawler had put the girl's good right arm into the sleeve of her own summer coat, a light fawn wool one she had taken with her inside the car, but had not worn. She used her. own brooch to fasten the coat over the sling.

"If you must get this case," she said, "You'd better have your dress covered and that shoulder. The dress is badly stained, you know."

Gwen nodded. Clearly she was making an immense effort, incapable of speaking or thinking, all her will and her courage bent upon getting into the bank. Mrs. Lawler, who had so far thought poorly of Gwen's qualities, was subdued by this near-heroism, and very ready to give all the help she could.

"Look," Owen breathed. "I've got to park the car. I can't wait here. Other side of the road, O.K.? Get the case. Then wait here by the steps."

"Ring for an ambulance," Mrs. Lawler said, giving

172

him a very hard look. "That's the first thing to be done, isn't it?"

He stared back at her.

"Of course," he said.

Gwen, still in the trance of her supreme effort, walked slowly to the correct grille, produced paper, passport and keys. While the case was being brought, Rose made her sit on one of the many upholstered benches, but when her property appeared, she got up at once and went forward to receive it. Mrs. Lawler caught her up.

"I'll carry it," she said.

"No."

"Don't be silly. Gwen. You're not fit . , ."

"I'm O.K."

No use struggling for possession Mrs. Lawler decided. The girl's beside herself, delirious perhaps. She managed to halve the weight of the case by slipping a couple of fingers into the handle beside Gwen's. In this fashion they reached the top of the three steps outside the door of the bank.

Owen was at the foot of them, waiting. He bounded up, snatched the case from the two women, held out his hand to Gwen.

"The key," he said, "Give me the key."

"No." She pulled back, shaking off Mrs. Lawler as well. "No, Owen! Not now. Not yet! Not . . ."

"I say yes," he snarled in a new voice that Rose had never heard before.

He tore the keys out of her hand, pulling her forward because she would not let go. She lost her balance, tripped on the next step and fell. As Rose jumped down to her side, Owen was away, running across the road to the car which he had parked as he intended, on the opposite side of the road in the shade of some trees.

Gwen lay where she had fallen. She began to cough, deep tearing coughs that made her cry out when she tried to take a breath. The coughing went on and now, to Mrs.

173

Lawler's horror, a dribble of blood-stained froth appeared at the corner of her mouth and grew — and grew — to a slow, persistent stream.

People stopped to stare and walk away or stay as their nature directed. The older among them found nothing altogether new in the spectacle. In the old days a tubercular haemorrhage from the lungs was less common than it had been in Victorian times, but still occurred in public from time to time. The sufferers from that age-old disease "consumption" still came to Switzerland in hope of a cure. Now the TB patients were cured, for the most part, in their own countries before such dire symptoms had a chance to develop.

But the younger passers-by stayed on. They saw the woman had not got the use of her left arm. An accident? An injury? Of course, the ambulance siren was sounding. What had happened inside the bank? Was it a hold-up? Had anyone heard a shot? Seen the thugs rush out?

Mrs. Lawler heard the siren too, with a feeling of great thankfulness. Owen had rung up after all. Her shock, horror even, at his callous, even brutal behaviour to Gwen, was swept away. She had misjudged him again. Poor Owen. In her relief at the restoration of her fantasy, she forgot to pity poor Gwen.

Her French was scarcely adequate to explain the position to the ambulance men, but they had no need for explanations. The woman on the pavement was coughing up blood. That was enough for them. They had Gwen on to a stretcher and into the ambulance in very quick time. As they were folding up the steps and preparing to close the doors Owen arrived beside them. He was carrying four suitcases which he handed over, saying briefly in Swiss German, "Their cases. Ya, it was I who rang you. Which hospital? Thanks I will follow."

The man nodded, fastened the doors, drove away.

Mrs. Lawler stood, holding Gwen's hand, watching the colour drain still further from her face, the grip on her own hand grow more feeble. She stared out of the back window of the ambulance. Yes, Owen was following. Why had she begun to distrust him? So suddenly, too. It was Gwen's fault for holding on to the keys. Why had she done that? What *was* this important suitcase, anyway?

Quite idly, she watched Owen keeping his place behind them. When another car intervened, she looked for Owen's car number, and afterwards found it at intervals until they had nearly reached the hospital, when with a twinge of conscience she saw for the first time that the ambulance man who had travelled inside with them was giving Gwen oxygen. After that her attention was wholly with the patient and continued so after the stretcher went inside. For the case had become very serious indeed, as she knew without being told. Suitcase or no suitcase, there ought to have been no delay. The injury was worse than either she or Owen had imagined. It might, she was told, be fatal. An immediate operation was necessary.

Only then did she look about for Owen. Only then did she learn that he had not arrived at the hospital.

"A man put these bags in the ambulance just outside the bank," the chief porter said. "For a Madame Lawlere, one of the ambulance men said."

He waited until she said, "I am Mrs. Lawler. Two bags are mine. These. The others belong to Mrs. Chilton."

She produced her passport. She took the passport from Gwen's handbag, which she had carried with her own from the steps of the bank and had kept with her own until this moment.

Now she looked inside the passport. It had an unfamiliar cover. She had seen Mrs. Chilton's British passport but never this thing. The photograph was of Gwen. The passport was Swiss: the name Geneviève Chillon.

Her suitcases were marked with the initials G.C. This seemed to satisfy both the porter and the ambulance men.

"I must stay until I have news of my friend," Mrs. Lawler told them in her heavily accented French.

"Bien entendu, madame," the porter answered politely. Another figure appeared behind Rose. He spoke in English much more fluent than her French.

"You are Madame Lawler?" he asked.

She still had the two passports in her hand. She offered them to the stranger.

"Yes," she answered. "Are you the police?"

The man looked at her with cold eyes.

"Madame expected it?"

"Now, yes. Until five minutes ago, no."

"Come with me, please."

She hesitated, seeing endless difficulty ahead.

"I do not speak French at all well — I think perhaps . . . the British Consul . . ."

"Come this way, please."

She followed, shaken by his persistence, fighting for time, to arrange her thoughts about Owen, about Gwen, about those presumably dead criminals, her would-be murderers.

"I must not leave the hospital until I have news of my friend, I must stay . . . speak to her when she is able to see me . . ."

A young man in a white coat came marching quickly to where she stood, half-way to the door. He spoke in French, but slowly, carefully.

"You are Madame Lawlere?"

She was tired of the repetition and replied sharply, "Yes. Why?"

"I have to tell you, with much regret, your friend has died."

"Oh *no*!"

"I regret. She was unconscious before the operation commenced. She did not survive it."

Poor Gwen. Poor silly, weak, criminal Gwen. Rose felt the tears well up behind her eyes. It was the porter who brought forward a chair. But Mrs. Lawler waved him back, turning to the first stranger.

"I will go with you," she said, "when you tell me who you are." And when he showed her his card and his authority she verified the truth of it first with the young doctor and then, for full measure, with the porter.

"I have our luggage," she said, pointing at the four suitcases. "They must go with me."

"Evidemment," he agreed and the porter took them to carry them out to the waiting police car.

"I regret . . . so much . . ." the doctor stammered.

"It was not your fault in any way," Mrs. Lawler told him, and turned and followed the porter through the open door, the police sergeant bringing up the rear.

Chapter XVIII

AT THE POLICE station Mrs. Lawler was put into a small bare room with a table in the middle and four stiff chairs against the walls. A policewoman guided her in, directing her to one of the chairs while she herself stood near the door with her back to it. Rose heard the door being locked on the outside.

So they think I am a criminal, too, she decided. Well, they have every excuse for that opinion. At present, until they hear my story. More important still, they must have time to establish that I really am the person I pretend to be.

Pretend. This should be easy in her own case, where there was no pretence at all. In fact she did not expect any difficulty over her own identity. But the others, all of the others, and her extraordinary involvement. How could anyone believe in it? Very deliberately Mrs. Lawler began to review in her own mind the long chain of events that had ended on the steps of the Swiss bank — no, later than that — at the hospital where Gwen had died and where Owen had not appeared.

So intent was Rose upon this process that she was quite startled to hear the door unlocked and to see a uniformed man who addressed her politely and asked her to follow him.

She was taken to a larger room, with a larger table,

really a desk, with papers, telephones, and other machines upon it. Behind the desk a more senior officer was sitting. Opposite him there was a much larger, more comfortable chair than the one in the small room. She was invited to sit in it. Her guide and the policewoman, still in attendance, retreated to chairs near the wall behind her.

The senior officer looked at her for a few seconds without speaking. Mrs. Lawler returned the look. Then he nodded.

"We were obliged to satisfy ourselves of your identity," he said at last, in very good English.

"Naturally," she answered and added, "I could not expect anything else."

He nodded again, clearly pleased by her manner and general appearance, since it fitted exactly with all he had so far heard about her.

"We know that your passport is correct in every particular. That you have been with an English touring party. That you left it at Venice, very early this morning, having given notice of your intention in writing in a note addressed to the courier, enclosed in a letter to one of the members of the tour."

"Mrs. Myra Donald, a member of the British Civil Service," Rose said, as the other paused.

"Just so. You went with another member of the tour, a Madame Geneviève Chillon . . ."

"I knew her as Mrs. Gwen Chilton. I also know that she had two passports. The Swiss one she used today and a British one."

Again he nodded, but went on.

"Also with a man, who drove the car, but was not a member of the tour."

"We met him first at Siena," Rose began, but the officer stopped her.

"I want you to tell me, in exact detail, the course of your drive to Geneva; where you stopped, all that happened on the way."

Mrs. Lawler protested.

"It won't mean anything until you know *why* I suddenly rushed away from the hotel on the Lido in the early hours. Not a thing I would ever think of doing . . ."

"I feel sure of that. Tell me, then, but as shortly as possible."

He leaned forward to switch on what she decided was a recording machine. Having already gone over her story so many times in her mind she gave it now without hesitation, in well-arranged detail, fluently. Seeing incredulity on all three faces in the room, she said, "Yes, I know it sounds like a fairy story, a Grimm's fairy story, but I *can* swim, you can verify that and those villains *exist* — or did exist."

The faces had relaxed, almost smiled, at the mention of Grimm, so she added, "You must remember I was a schoolmistress — sports and gymnasium — I was trained to think and act quickly in physical ways and to teach children to do that."

"I am sure you succeeded admirably," the chief officer said with a little bow. "So proceed, Mrs. Lawler, from the time of leaving Venice."

She gave a very clear account of it all, including her failed watch on Gwen, the assumed betrayal, the scene on the mountain, Gwen's insistence upon not going to hospital until she had recovered her property at the bank.

"You already knew this woman was a criminal and an associate of criminals. When did you first suspect this?"

She told him then the full story of Gwen's attempt to steal her photographs and all that lay behind it. She disclosed the whereabouts of all her photographs; she suggested that Mr. Banks might add to the story of Gwen's activities. All the time she brought Owen as little as possible into the story, but she could not conceal the fact that he had added to Gwen's injury by pulling her down the steps at the bank.

"And failing to appear at the hospital?"

"Yes. But he put all our cases into the ambulance."

"After taking the one from the deposit over to the car, where no doubt he looked inside it and found nothing to his liking, perhaps. Perhaps some money. We may never know."

"I don't understand."

"I do not intend at the moment that you should. It would help us if you can give me a closer description of this man. Also of his car."

"I never know the makes of cars."

"The number?"

"Oh yes, that was . . ."

She stopped, remembering perfectly that she had watched the car's progress through the traffic. Why did they want to know? Clearly Owen had meant to steal Gwen's case but had changed his mind because she was ill. Dying, her conscience told her. But still . . .

"Well, Mrs. Lawler. The number?"

"I think Owen was not altogether honest," she said, stalling. "But this time he gave back the case when perhaps he meant to take it."

The officer was angry.

"He gave it back because he knew he couldn't use the stuff in it. He gave it back because he knew he'd killed the girl and he had to get out quick."

"*He* killed her! It was Abe! I told you — with the gun in Jake's car, leaning out of the window. Firing . . ."

"Mrs. Lawler," the officer said, "I have a report from the hospital. It tallies with the account you have just given me. The woman was lying on her face with her feet up the road towards you. You have said this. The shot, then, had thrown her *forward*, not stopped her from in front. The wound of entry of the bullet was in her back, the wound you dressed was the wound of exit. No, I do not blame you. You could not see how it was. You did not examine. He would not have allowed it."

She shuddered. It explained many things. That Owen had worked only for himself from start to finish. That he

181

had not meant to kill Gwen, only stop her from joining those others and then destroy them.

"Gwen was not really very ill at first," Rose said. "I'm sure he only meant to stop her helping Jake, joining him again. Until she fell down the steps . . ."

"That was his doing as you describe it. The medical report shows the apex of the lung was injured by the bullet and was probably further torn by the fall and displacement of the pad you put on the wound. She died from severe haemorrhage of the lung."

So he was the murderer. Oh Owen, Owen, she mourned, bending her head in sorrow and shame for him.

"I will give you the number of his car," she said at last.

After that Mrs. Lawler was taken to another room where a more senior policewoman attended her with great kindness and consideration. Her suitcases were brought in, a police doctor came to see her, advised a hot drink and sedation. She was asked to wait a little longer in order to help the inquiries that were going forward with all speed. There was a couch in the room. The policewoman got Rose to lie down on it and covered her up. She slept for four hours.

At the end of that time, which she saw by her watch was still as early as eleven o'clock of the same night, of the same unending day, she roused herself to sit up and look about her. Yet another policewoman was now in attendance, jumping up at once to ask if there was anything she wanted. This one spoke in French, seemed not to understand English, Rose found, but did gather that she wanted first a wash, then something to drink. For her mouth was almost too dry for speech and her head ached abominably.

The policewoman took her to a bathroom which was also a lavatory, gave her a clean towel and left her to lock herself in. So they were treating her now more as a visitor than a criminal, Rose decided. Or perhaps chiefly as a

182

fairly valuable informer. She expected to find her escort outside the door when she unlocked it and in this she was right. They went back to the room where she had slept and directly afterwards a young police officer came in with a tray of food, a bowl of excellent soup, some fresh rolls, cheese and fruit.

Mrs. Lawler drank the soup very thankfully, but had little appetite for anything else. There was too much she wanted to know but feared she would never be told. As before her chief anxiety was Owen. She did not, could never as long as she lived, forgive him for killing Gwen, but he had not meant to kill, nor even to wound severely. Of that she was certain. He was greedy for money and — other things — Gwen, for instance. But he was not violent, nor brutal. She had closed her mind to those moments, when an evil stranger took over the kind eyes, the gentle speech. He had suffered in his youth, too much, like Charles; he had not been helped to find a new life. And now she had betrayed him, because Gwen had died and he was wanted as her murderer.

She had barely finished her meal when the young policeman came back to take away her tray and speak privately to the policewoman. The latter then said, speaking in very stilted English, "You will come, please, madame."

"Of course," Rose answered, wondering what the next interview would demand or disclose, hoping it would be the last and she would be allowed to go away to a hotel for the night, after booking a place on a plane to England in the morning.

She was taken to the same room where her earlier interview had been held. The same senior Swiss police officer was there and with him two other men, not in uniform but in suits so clearly English in cut, colour and style that her heart rose in instant thankfulness. With no surprise she was introduced to the local British consul and to Chief Detective Superintendent Wonersh of the Fraud Squad at Scotland Yard.

"That name will perhaps explain," the Swiss said as they all sat down.

"Not altogether," Mrs. Lawler answered. "But I take it Superintendent Wonersh has something to do with the contents of poor Gwen's deposit case?"

"You take it correctly," the Superintendent said, smiling

"May I know?"

"Not the detail, I'm afraid."

"I shouldn't understand that, I'm sure."

"Perhaps. In any case, it is only part of a big operation being attempted by an American fraud gang, using forged share certificates, forged currency, forged travellers' cheques and so on. The particular offshoot that concerned the woman you knew as Mrs. Chilton is, or was, only one of several. The overall boss or bosses have never appeared this side of the Atlantic. The man you knew as Jake, with Gwen and a varying bodyguard, has been operating between England and the Continent for several years. She was originally English which is how we began six months ago to trace how they worked."

"But she's dead," Rose said. "And so are those thugs. Surely?" She turned to the Swiss officer. "Surely you know this now, don't you?"

"We have found a car and three bodies," he answered. "I hope you will be willing to identify them."

As she recoiled from this prospect the consul said, "It is a request, Mrs. Lawler, which I hope you will decide to meet. Seeing that you have done such a truly magnificent action in breaking up this gang and indeed disposing of them."

"Very well," she answered. "But it wasn't only me. There were other people on the tour who saw Jake. And a Mr. Banks, who noticed Gwen in the bank at San Gimignano."

"Where she used her Swiss passport," the Superintendent said. "Among other useful information the tourists gave this evening at Cremona, Mrs. Lawler. Mr. Banks

184

was particularly helpful in regard to Mr. Strong, as you call him."

Rose, who had been hoping all the talk about the international fraud plot had put any further questions about Owen out of their minds, was disappointed by this, and then blamed herself for her still lingering hopes for his escape. In her mind she now called his action unintentional, unpremeditated manslaughter.

"In what way?" she asked.

"General suspicion," Wonersh answered, looking at her very sternly. "Our colleagues in Cremona got nothing definite from Mr. Banks except suspicion of the way the man Strong was following Mrs. Chilton from place to place. With intent, he said."

No need to ask what sort of intent, Rose thought. She knew the kind of intent a Mr. Banks had in mind. Most of the tour people also. What a flutter in 'Roseanna' tonight! Poor Myra and Flo! Thank God she wasn't there.

After a few moments of silence the consul said, "Shall we go, Mrs. Lawler?"

"*Go?*"

"To the mortuary."

"Oh! Oh, yes."

The Swiss police officer again apologised for submitting her to this ordeal.

"But you have shown such outstanding courage, madame. You have defeated single-handed, and exposed completely, a most important set of criminals. Your country and mine are so grateful. I am sure . . ."

She could not bear it. She had escaped from the launch by her own action, but for the rest she had relied on Owen. He had saved her from Jake on the road at the Furka Pass.

Useless to point this out to them. Useless, really, to persuade herself of the real truth of the matter. That ruined face still haunted her.

She got up, saying briefly, "Let us go, then."

185

The identification was managed very discreetly, very calmly. Jake's ugly face had not been mutilated in his death. His crushed-in skull did not show from the front of his head. There was no difficulty at all for her. She moved from Jake's body to that of Abe. Here there was a difference: a hole in the man's forehead; the bullet must have killed him instantly.

"I suppose Owen shot him," she said. "I didn't see, I was face down on the road near Gwen. But this man was leaning out of their car window with a levelled gun."

"We have the gun," the Swiss officer said. "We recovered it from where it had been thrown down the hill after the car. There was also a bullet hole in one front tyre and skid marks on the road. But this gun had not been fired."

They left the mortuary. The Swiss officer again thanked Mrs. Lawler, shook her hand, told her the English Superintendent Wonersh would explain more to her and the consul would look after her.

The consul said, "My car should be around here by now. There it is."

Wonersh said, "May I come with you? I think we do owe Mrs. Lawler a little more information."

She did not understand what he meant until they were all three in the consul's private house to which he had driven them. Then, when they were all sitting comfortably in his study the consul said, "I have brought you here, Mrs. Lawler, partly to explain that I have already been able to book you a seat on a plane tomorrow — well, today it is now — partly because I hope you will allow my wife and me to put you up overnight, what there is left of it, and partly so that Superintendent Wonersh here can give you more detail about the man you know as Owen Strong." He held his hand up as she began to protest. "No, please. I have heard the tape recordings of your adventure at Venice. And of the appearance of this man earlier in your trip. I think you ought to know more of him. I'm afraid you are in some way blaming yourself for his behaviour. Mr. Wonersh will tell you this is quite unnecessary."

"I know he is what you call bent," she said, still defiant, looking at the Superintendent.

"Very bent, Mrs. Lawler," Wonersh began. "Good professional stock, third in a family of four, two boys, two girls. Happy home, good school, average learner, average at sports. Began to steal at school, but got away with it by adding blackmail if anyone accused him. Enough leaked, however, for him to be sacked — expelled, they called it then."

"How old is he really?" Rose asked.

"Born 1915. Father in wartime job at home. Over forty. Not called up."

"Fifty-eight, then. About what I thought. Go on."

She was very calm. It all fitted. In his twenties in the second war, like Charles.

"After the disaster at school he went out to cousins in Canada where he stayed just six months before they threw him out, with a ticket for a ship home.

He sold the ticket and went to the States. We have no detail but he kept himself by his wits, by which I mean his crimes, with very few arrests and convictions and only very short sentences or fines. Until he enlisted in the U.S. forces and came to England with a part of their Air Force."

"The U.S. Air Force," Rose broke in again. "He told me that, but I thought he meant the R.A.F. A pilot, of course."

"By no means." The Superintendent for the first time allowed contempt to creep into his voice. "In the catering department at one of their Air Fields in England. From which he was duly fired for attempted blackmail and theft from the mess. We have no record for the rest of the war, but later, after it was over, he turned up on the French Riviera, playing his old games, chiefly blackmail. He plays it carefully, I understand, always on the better class victim who can afford a reasonable sum but who has no means of rubbing him out, as a tycoon might. People almost never try to shop him, because of the scandal. He plays France, Italy, and also Switzerland, where he can pick up other villains stashing their gains in the very private deposits they go in for over here. As this Jake did, through Gwen. Her real name was Mabel Smith, incidentally. Failed actress on third-rate tour in the States, but English. Manager of the tour scarpered, leaving them all broke. Asset to Jake and too dim ever to leave him, I gather from their records. Even through his prison sentences."

He paused, looking at Rose, who seemed puzzled, no longer listening carefully. Presently she said, turning an anxious face in his direction, "Have they stopped Owen? Have they arrested him?"

"Not yet. The car whose number you gave, was picked up in the town here, abandoned. It was checked out with the car-hire firm in Venice. He had hired it in the name of Culver. He was registered at the hotel on the Lido as Culver."

"I see." She did indeed see now how he had managed to stay at the tour hotel unseen and unknown to them all.

"He had a great many aliases," the Superintendent went on. "Strong, Culver, Martindale ... His real name is John Fareham."

"So where is he now?" she asked.

"Who knows? Probably borrowed or stolen another car and is out of Switzerland into France to hide up while the heat is on. The frontier is very close to Geneva. He might be anywhere. But for the first time he is no longer a nuisance, as he has been. He is a murderer, a wanted murderer. And with that face of his ..."

"Yes," Mrs. Lawler said. "That face. That scarred face. He *must* have flown in the war to get that face. Burned. A pilot, shot down ..."

She could not go on.

"*No*," Wonersh said in a voice that made her stare at

him in amazement. "I am sorry to upset your romantic conclusion, Mrs. Lawler, but this so-called Owen got those scars in a gang fight in Chicago, soon after the war on the only visit he ever made back to the States. Acid burns, thrown acid, not war wounds at all."

She covered her face with her hands, then deliberately took them away to tell them how Charles, her husband, had been burned, how he had survived, how he had died. How she had felt pity for a like victim, not romantic, but a fool all the same, an old fool.

"Not at all. Very natural," the consul said, highly embarrassed.

But Superintendent Wonersh, who had a deeper knowledge of the strange twists and turns of guilt in its endlessly various forms, was not embarrassed. He said carefully, "I'm sure we none of us misunderstood your apparent regard for Owen, Mrs. Lawler. Perhaps you have always blamed yourself too much for your husband's suicide. If you will forgive me, I think he must have been a very vain man to be unable to stand his altered appearance. Not much consideration for you when you were expecting his child. Those skin grafts in the war settled down wonderfully in a lot of cases. In time, you know. I've seen them."

He stopped, partly because Mrs. Lawler was crying quietly now, relieved at last of a great measure of the old grief she had forced into remorse. The Superintendent did not try to comfort her, but the consul suddenly jumped to his feet, saying "God bless my soul! The cable!" and rushed from the room.

As Rose understood a little later, the various inquiries in England and with the tour had revealed a cable waiting to be delivered to her the next day at Gatwick on her return. It was to the effect that her son and his wife would be flying over the following day and hoped to meet her at Heathrow, apologies for short notice and love.

189

Rose was overwhelmed. She could not wait. She must go at once. *At once.*

"But you must rest a bit," the consul's wife implored.

"Rest!" Mrs. Lawler could not find word for her impatience.

But the Superintendent said, "You can come with me, Mrs. Lawler. Plane at 1.30 a.m. Heathrow. My other chap here can swop tickets with you. Get your things and we'll go off to the airport at once."

"The woman's been up for over forty-eight hours without a break," the consul protested as his wife took the excited Rose from the room.

"Policemen and doctors do it frequently," was all the answer he had to that.

"She's over sixty! She'll throw a heart attack on you in the plane!"

"Not she. Tough as old boots," Wonersh said with conviction. "She'll meet that selfish son of hers right on time at Heathrow. Takes after his father, I shouldn't wonder."